The Frannie Shoemaker Campground Series

Bats and Bones

The Blue Coyote

Peete and Repeat

The Lady of the Lake

To Cache a Killer

Also by Karen Musser Nortman

The Time Travel Trailer

Happy Camper Tips and Recipes

to cache a killer

killer

A Frannie Shoemaker
Campground Mystery

by Karen Musser Nortman

Cover Artwork by Aurora Lightbourne
Cover Design by Libby Shannon

Dedicated to campers and geocachers everywhere

TABLE OF CONTENTS

INTRODUCTION

GEOCACHING IS AN outdoor treasure hunting game made possible in the last decade by hand-held GPS devices. According to Geocaching.com, over six million people worldwide currently participate in trying to find two and a half million caches.

A geocache is a weatherproof container ranging in size from very small (a 35 mm film canister) to quite large (a bucket.) At the minimum, it contains paper and a pencil so that finders can log their user name and the date. It may also contain trade items or trackable items. If a trade item is taken out by the finder, it must be replaced with an item of equal value. A trackable item is intended to be moved to another cache in order to complete a certain journey and includes a number which allows the geocacher to log the item on line and receive instructions on where it should go.

Caches are hidden in places that are accessible with the permission of land owners or managers but where geocachers will not cause damage to the environment or be seen by non-geocachers (muggles.) They may be in places like a hollow tree, under debris on the ground, or even in a magnetic container on the back of a road sign or on a bridge support.

Caches are listed by their GPS coordinates on the geocaching website. The geocacher enters the location where they wish to search by zip code or other identifier and a list of caches in that area appears. The geocacher selects the caches he or she wishes to find and enters the coordinates in a GPS device or a GPS-enabled mobile phone. The hunt is on. The geocacher not only signs the log in the cache, but also records the find or failure on the website.

Geocaching is challenging and a good excuse for a hike. More information can be found at www.geocaching.com.

CHAPTER ONE
THURSDAY AFTERNOON

"CAN YOU REACH it?"

Frannie Shoemaker swatted a mosquito targeting her eye and felt her left foot slip on the loose rocks. She grabbed at a small tree growing out of the rock wall and avoided a tumble, but not the somersaults in her stomach. She glanced back at Mickey, her brother-in-law, behind and below her. Inadvertently her eyes took in the drop down the hillside they had just climbed. What had she been thinking when she made the climb up? That she would be beamed back down?

"Frannie?"

"Shut up, Mick." She gritted her teeth and turned back to the crevice just barely at her eye level. "Even if I reach it, how are we going to sign the log? I can't let go to write or even open it."

"I can. Hand it down to me."

"I need something to pull it out." She let go of the tree with her right hand, and still gripping the rocks with her left, pressed against the cliff with her whole body and wiped her sweaty hand on her jeans. "Have you got a stick?"

"Here."

She felt a nudge on her hand and clasped a sturdy round piece of wood. The weight of it pulled at her balance. "Is that your walking stick?"

"Sure is. Glad to share."

Frannie let go of the stick and heard it clatter back down the hill. She grabbed the tree again, the rough bark a comfort. "That's too long, you numbskull! I can't maneuver that. Find a short stick."

"Geesh. Next time I'm going to partner with someone who's not so crabby. You should have let me go first. I—"

"Shut up, Mick," she said again, her breath coming in short gasps, and changed tones. "*Please*, find me a smaller stick."

"That's better. Don't be so scared. If you slip, I'll catch you."

"Ha! If I slip, we'll both end up at the bottom, smashed on the rocks."

"Thanks for the vote of confidence. Try this." Mickey placed a sturdy twig in her hand.

It was about eighteen inches long. Frannie carefully raised it to the level of the crevice without backing her body away from the wall even an inch. Using the hooked end like a claw, she managed to pull the small plastic box closer to the edge of the crevice. She dropped the stick and grabbed the box, handing it down to Mickey without looking. "Here. Open it and sign the log and I'll put it back. Then we can get down from here."

"And I thought Jane Ann was bossy," Mickey grumbled but took the box from her. She heard him unsnap the lid. "Hey, look, there's a travel bug in here. I've never found one of those."

"I'll look later, okay?" Frannie said weakly. She was torn between wanting off the side of this steep hillside and fearing the actual descent. "Put the travel bug in your pocket. We have to log the number online."

In a minute, Mickey had scratched his name and the date on a small strip of paper, returned it and the stubby pencil to the box, snapped it closed, and handed it back.

Frannie placed it in the crevice and pushed it back as far as she could. "It's not as far as it was, but it's close," she said.

"G o o d   e n o u g h," M i c k e y   s a i d   i n   a n uncharacteristically serious tone. "Now I'll guide you down to that last ledge and then you'll be able to take the path. Move your right foot straight down about eight inches. There's a root there."

Frannie realized that Mickey finally understood how frightened she was. She did as she was told and step by step descended the ten feet or so to the narrow path. Coming up, she had thought that path the worst route she had ever taken. Now it was a safe haven compared to the steep hillside.

"Put one hand on my shoulder," Mickey said.

Frannie did so with her left hand and wiped the tree sap off her right hand so she could use it to grope along the wall.

"Owww!" Mickey flinched. "I said put your hand on my shoulder, not grip with a death claw!"

5

"Sorry." She relaxed her hand and they proceeded down the path. Mickey's solid, squat body not only gave her confidence but also blocked her view of the steep descent. She kept her eyes fixed on the ground immediately in front of her feet.

"Slow down, please," Frannie said. He did.

Mickey slowed. "I sure hope we can find my walking stick at the bottom," he said. "That was a good one."

"I'll buy you a new one if we don't. Just get me down from here safely."

"'Course if I had a Corvette, I wouldn't need a walking stick."

"Shut up."

"You say that a lot."

The banter continued as they picked their way down to the bottom of the ravine. Frannie let out a deep breath, collapsed on a boulder, and unclipped the water bottle that she carried attached to a belt loop. She took a swig and offered it to Mickey.

Mickey looked at her. "Man, you are all sweaty! Your hair is soaking wet."

She ran her fingers through damp curls. "Nice girls don't sweat...or something like that."

"It's not even warm today."

"Nerves, Mickey. Sixty-five is too old for this and I never did like heights. I'm surprised they don't take your Geocaching login away when you start collecting Social Security."

"But we found it." He patted his pocket. "Maybe the others didn't do so well."

She cocked her head at him. "Have you considered that all of the rest are in much better shape than you and me? And that we probably got the hardest one?"

"There's that," Mickey said.

"Let me see the Travel Bug. Is there anything with it?" She held out her hand.

He pulled a shiny metal tag, like a dog tag, from his pocket and gave it to her. The attached keychain was looped through a small piece of green plastic. Examining it closely, she said, "I think it's one of those Ninja turtle things." She handed it back.

"So what do we do with it, do you know?"

"See the number on the tag? When we log our find on the website, we can enter that number and find out where it's been and what the goal is. Sometimes the owner wants it to go around the world or to a certain state or something. So we have to place it in another cache to get it closer to its goal."

She got up and brushed off the seat of her jeans. "We should probably get back to the cars. I'll bet the others are done."

"I gotta find my stick first." Mickey turned and headed back along the ravine to the area below the crevice where they had found the geocache.

Frannie followed. When she caught up, Mickey was pawing through some shrubs at the side of the ravine. Frannie looked around on the ground and then her eyes traveled up the side of the hill.

"Uh, Mick."

He stopped thrashing around and looked up to where she was pointing.

"What?"

"There, in that pine."

Protruding out of the top of a scrubby white pine about twenty feet up the slope was the polished end of Mickey's walking stick.

"How did it do that?"

Frannie shrugged. "It must have bounced. Or something."

Mickey picked up a small rock and aimed it at the stick. It hit the pine but didn't dislodge the stick. After several more fruitless tries, he sighed.

"I'll need to come back with better equipment."

"Like what?"

"A bigger stick."

"I'm really sorry, Mickey. I really will buy you a new one if you want."

"I'm not giving up yet. C'mon, let's go find the others."

Frannie had relaxed enough from her harrowing climb to enjoy their hike back up the ravine to the car park. Dolomite State Park, named for the striking limestone formations, remained one of Frannie's all-time favorites for camping. She had cooled off after the tension of the climb, almost to the point of chills, but now the spring sun and the walk warmed her and it was welcome. Occasional violets peeked through spots on the leaf-covered ground, like feeble forays of civilization into this prehistoric looking place. The pitted grey rock resembled old bones as much as anything. Fragile light green leaves made a brave showing on spindly shrubs as the base of the cliff.

As they neared the car park, she could make out the slender form of her sister-in-law, Jane Ann, sitting on the hood of the Shoemaker pickup, and their friend and fellow camper, Ben Terell, leaning against his own truck, arms crossed and laughing. Jane Ann saw them coming and waved.

When Frannie got close, Jane Ann said to her, "You look like you've been wrestling a bear. Where did my crazy husband lead you?"

"Gee, thanks," Frannie said. To her surprise, Mickey came to her defense.

"It was a really steep climb. She didn't want to, but she went all the way up and found it."

"Ohhh," Jane Ann said. The whole group was well aware of how Frannie felt about high places. She slid off the truck hood and put her arm around Frannie's shoulders. "I'm sorry, sweetie. Make that lazy brother of mine cook you supper tonight."

Mickey scoffed. "We guys are cooking anyway."

Ben said, "So you and Frannie found your cache?"

Mickey pulled the travel bug out of his pocket. "And one of these. Did you guys find yours?"

"Yup," Ben said. "It was a pretty easy one. But no travel bug. Let me see that."

"How about Larry and Nancy? Have you seen them?"

"Not yet," Ben said. "But we saw a group of Boy Scouts and I'll bet Nancy had to stop and organize them." They all laughed, knowing Nancy's penchant for getting things in order.

Frannie and Jane Ann watched a family with young kids at a nearby shelter and reminisced about camping with their own kids. Mickey showed Ben the travel bug. They waited about ten minutes before Frannie's husband Larry and Nancy Terell appeared.

"Finally!" Mickey said. "Took you long enough."

Nancy made a face. "And we didn't even find it."

"Really?" Jane Ann said.

"It was supposed to be by that spring," Larry said, rubbing his crew cut. "Must have been moved."

"Oh, right. Nancy, you just need a better partner," Mickey said.

"Zip it, Ferraro," Larry said.

"Somebody's a sore loser," Frannie whispered to Jane Ann, garnering a dirty look from her husband.

"Mickey and Frannie found a travel bug in theirs," Jane Ann said.

Larry perked up. "Cool," he said, looking at Frannie.

She held up her hands. "I have the limestone dust under my fingernails to prove it."

Mickey proceeded to give a blow-by-blow account, slightly embellished, of their climb and the loss of his favorite walking stick.

"Congratulations, m'dear," Larry said. He knew how difficult such a climb would be for her. "What's the plan? More of this nonsense or back to camp?"

"Mickey says you guys are cooking tonight, so you'll probably need all the time you can get," Jane Ann said.

"I'm ready to settle my nerves," Frannie said. "Besides, I want to see what we can find out about this travel bug."

Ben started his truck. "We can continue this contest tomorrow." Nancy and Mickey climbed in with him while the others got in Larry's truck. The road back to the campground area of the park was, although winding, paved so Frannie only needed to keep herself stabilized side-to-side. Conservative in most things, Larry sometimes forgot when driving that he wasn't in a patrol car in hot pursuit any more. The trees overhanging the road were just beginning to show evidences of gauzy spring green.

"So what's for supper? You guys have been keeping it a big secret."

Larry waggled his eyebrows. "I'm sworn not to tell. I'm afraid of Mickey."

"Hah!" said his sister. "You're doing the sides and everything?"

"Everything. It is our pleasure to serve the lovely ladies in our lives."

"Oh, brother," Frannie said.

"That's my line," Jane Ann told her.

Chapter Two
Late Thursday Afternoon

THE CAMPGROUND SAT at one of the highest points in the park. The Shoemakers, Terells, and Ferraros had spacious sites in a row shaded by several hard maples and oaks. The space between Ferraros' red and white Class C motorhome and Shoemakers' thirty-foot trailer had been chosen as the gathering spot for their group.

"We're cooking in the Red Rocket," Larry said, nodding toward Jane Ann and Mickey's motorhome. "So you girls have to entertain yourself elsewhere."

"No problem," Frannie said. "Mickey, give me the travel bug and we'll check it out."

"How do you live with this woman?" Mickey said to Larry, as he handed over the tag.

"I just do what she says."

Frannie rolled her eyes and led Jane Ann and Nancy into her trailer. Her laptop was charging on the dinette and the list of area geocaches was still on the screen. Frannie located the cache that she and Mickey had found and entered the date. Then she went to the trackables page and Nancy read the number off the tag while Frannie typed it in.

"Hence the name—Construction Project," Nancy said.

"It has a low difficulty rating." Frannie looked at her watch. "Since the guys are doing supper, we could go find it now."

"Excellent," Nancy said. "I'll drive, but I need to walk Chloe first."

"Same with Cuba," Frannie said. The old yellow Lab raised her head from the floor where she had been curled up since they walked in. Her ears perked up at her name.

Jane Ann still had her Garmin GPS device on a strap around her neck, so took it off and entered the coordinates.

"We could have just downloaded them," Frannie said.

Jane Ann just shrugged. "I always forget that."

They trooped out of the trailer and Nancy went to get her Boston terrier/beagle mix, Chloe, while Frannie hooked Cuba up on her leash. They walked around one loop of the campground. The afternoon was fresh with spring ready to burst. There were a lot of empty campsites but this was only Thursday. By tomorrow night at this time, the campground would be full.

Returning to their own sites, they passed a couple working near a popup trailer with a Kentucky license plate a few spaces down from them. The woman looked up and motioned for them to wait.

"Hi," she said, as she ambled toward the road. "I have a question. Do you guys have power?"

"Yes, we do. Why?" Frannie said.

"Ours doesn't seem to be working," the woman said. She pushed her light brown hair back from her face and looked back at their site. "Must be our post then—better talk to the ranger. We had power earlier today. Thanks." She turned and walked back toward her companion.

When they returned Nancy put Chloe in her trailer and walked over to Ferraros'. She yelled through the screen door, "Ben!"

"You can't come in!" Mickey yelled back.

"I just need the keys to the truck," Nancy said. "We're going to go look for another cache."

Ben appeared at the door with Mickey and Larry looking over his shoulders. "How come?"

Frannie held up the travel bug and explained what the instructions were.

"Since we're not doing anything, we thought we could get a head start on finding the rest."

Ben nodded and opened the door to hand the keys out. "Supper's in an hour."

"Hour and a half," Mickey said.

"Better make it two hours," Larry said.

The women laughed, took the keys and headed for Terell's yellow truck. The campground road led to the south entrance of the park. Nancy turned left onto a county gravel road that led them back into the park farther north. A few more turns and they arrived at the museum dedicated to the history of the CCC in Iowa. The limestone building with dark wood trim looked deserted and a sign on the door said closed.

"I think it's only open on weekends," Nancy said. She parked and they climbed out of the truck. Jane Ann turned on the GPS and waited for it to connect with a satellite.

"Back that way," she said, pointing behind the building. An expanse of grass led to a small creek that separated the lawn from the limestone bluffs. The late afternoon sun cast long shadows, but where it broke through, the freshly mowed grass was emerald green and the scent was intoxicating. Jane Ann led, keeping one eye on the screen of the GPS.

"One hundred feet."

When she reported that they were within five feet, they fanned out, searching along the creek bank.

After a bit, Frannie said, "You know, if it was down low, it would likely get washed away when the creek floods. So it must be up off the ground."

"Oh, you are so smart," Nancy said. So they began searching in the shrubs and small trees on the bank.

"What does the GPS show, Jane Ann?" Frannie said.

"You know how it goes. When I stand right here, it says it's three feet to the left. But when I move that direction, it says it's six feet behind me. Not very accurate when you get close."

Nancy chose a spot in the center of the area Jane Ann had indicated. "Okay, we need to start from here and each of us work our way out in different directions. Once we get out about five or six feet, we each circle to our left until we've covered the area. If we don't find it, we'll work farther out."

"Until we fall in the creek?" Jane Ann asked with a smirk.

"Yeah, Nancy, then what?" Left to herself, Frannie would have just wandered around the area, but such disorganization was anathema to Nancy.

Nancy grinned. "I will stop you before you fall in the creek, I promise."

So like triple duelers, they stood back to back at the spot Nancy had chosen.

"I bet we look like 'Charlie's Angels,'" Frannie said.

"In your dreams," Jane Ann said.

They carefully watched the ground around their feet and examined small shrubs as they moved out from the center. Nancy ordered a halt and directed them to each move to their left.

"And do-si-do your partner," Jane Ann called out.

Frannie moved toward a pile of rocks. Some elderberry bushes separated the rocks from the creek.

"What?" Frannie blurted, and stopped, staring at the rocks.

"What what?" Nancy said.

Frannie pointed between the rocks and the shrubs. Her voice came out kind of squeaky. "A shoe."

"Oh, no." Jane Ann's voice was low, wary. Only the sole of the shoe could be seen protruding from the rocks.

"Surely not," Jane Ann continued and looked at Frannie.

Nancy prodded the shoe with a stick and it tumbled off the rocks.

Frannie let a breath out and put a hand to her chest. "No one attached. Thank goodness." She began to look closer at a small serviceberry tree in the midst of the elderberries. Reaching up, she pulled a pinecone out of the crotch of the tree.

"Not many pine trees around here." She turned it over to reveal a flat bottom with a rectangular panel printed with the words *Official Geocache – Please do not remove* and some symbols.

"Aha!" she said and pried the back off while Nancy and Jane Ann gathered close. Inside was a tiny metal tube with a lid.

"No Ninja Turtles are going to fit in there," Jane Ann said.

Frannie unscrewed the top and pulled out a small roll of paper. "You're right. Nothing else in there." She signed the log with the stubby pencil, replaced it, and replaced the back.

Nancy put it back in the tree and they ambled back to the truck.

When they returned to the campground, the picnic table had been covered with a flowered vinyl cloth and set with bright plastic plates. A large tomato sauce can in the center held a bouquet of daisies.

"Wow!" Nancy said. "Flowers even."

"Wonder where they stole those?" Jane Ann said.

Mickey descended the motorhome steps balancing a cast iron Dutch oven.

"Didn't steal nothin'. I had to go to town for a couple of things and they had those in the grocery store.

17

Perfectly legal daisies." He marched over to the fire pit and carefully balanced the pot on the swinging grill. He stood back up and turned to the women. "Did you find anything?"

"We thought for a minute that Frannie found another body," Jane Ann said.

"Oh, hush. It was just a shoe. The body thing has only happened a couple of times and it wasn't just me. Anyway, we found the cache but no turtles."

"Let's go log it," Nancy said. "And look at that list again. You know, we can eliminate any of the real small ones. I didn't think of that before. How long 'til supper?"

"About an hour," Mickey said.

"That's what you told us when we left," Frannie said.

"What can I say? Perfection takes time. It would be easier to gauge the time if I had one of those Dutch oven cooking tables."

"Mickey, if you had any more cooking equipment, we would have to get a bigger motorhome," Jane Ann said.

"We could just get a trailer to pull behind," he said.

"No," said Jane Ann. "Quit whining."

He sighed dramatically and returned to his camper, where the women could hear Larry and Ben arguing.

"I don't even want to know what that's about. C'mon." Frannie led the way back into her trailer.

The women perused the list of nearby caches. Nancy pointed out another one that was listed as a nano cache— too small for a turtle. They picked out two more caches in the park, the one in the cemetery and one in the nearest town as the best possibilities, and Frannie wrote the names down.

"Don't forget the one Larry and I didn't find," Nancy said. "Spring Ahead. Tomorrow maybe we can split into two teams and concentrate on those five."

Frannie got a bottle of pinot grigio out of the refrigerator and some plastic wine glasses. "Sounds like we might as well relax for a while."

They went back outside and Nancy brought a plate of pita chips and bowl of humus dip out of her trailer. Jane Ann and Frannie were already in their lawn chairs and dove into the dip while they watched as the scattering of other occupied campsites bustled with supper activity. The women commented on a couple of fifth wheels in the next loop and discussed a dispute going on in the local city council back home. They brought each other up to date on their children and watched their husbands scurry in and out with bowls and spoons. Frannie relished the relaxed atmosphere in the midst of activity. This was what camping was all about.

"Kind of remind you of the Oompa Loompas, don't they," Jane Ann said, nodding toward their husbands.

Frannie chuckled. "This better be worth it."

Mickey came back out to fuss with his Dutch oven, carefully holding the lid to shield the contents so the women couldn't see into the pot.

"How long now, Mickey? About an hour?"

"Go ahead and laugh," Mickey said. "You will regret your cruelty when you savor this dish. And for your information, it should be ready in ten minutes."

It was more like twenty minutes, but the group finally sat at the table and refreshed their wine glasses for a toast.

"To us!" Ben said, raising his glass. "And to our lovely wives, who are so fortunate to have such talented and attentive mates."

"Hear, hear!" Larry and Mickey chimed in.

"That remains to be seen. But we'll give you the benefit of the doubt," Jane Ann said, and the women joined the toast.

Mickey produced a platter of Parmesan chicken, perfectly done. Bowls of noodles, roasted Brussels sprouts, and fresh fruit were passed. Larry sliced a loaf of French bread and everyone dug in.

"I got a text from Maury Brenton while we were cooking. Bones Lemming resigned from the city council," Mickey said.

"Really?" Frannie said. "We were just talking about the water dispute."

Ben cocked his head. "Sounds like a chopper."

They looked up. "National Guard training maybe? Or Medevac?" Larry said.

"There it is," Nancy said, pointing to the northern sky.

They returned to their meal with gusto.

"I have to say, guys, this is awesome. So good that I think you should do all of the cooking from now on," Frannie said around a mouthful.

"Bad manners," Larry said. "Your mother would not have been pleased." He stopped and listened. "Sirens."

"Must be an accident or something," Nancy said.

"Tell us about the cache you found." Ben put down his fork to start the chicken around again.

Frannie explained in detail the instructions with the tracking bug and how they planned to continue the search.

"So if we don't find them all, we have to put the ones we did find back?" Mickey said.

"Yes and that means it will be your job to return the one we found. No way I'm going to make that climb again."

Mickey put on a pout. "Wouldn't be so bad if I had my walking stick."

"Zip it. I'm sorry about the stick but I did ask for a stick to pull the cache out with. Why would you think I could use one that big?"

"I didn't know how far back it was," Mickey complained.

"If it had been that far back, I wouldn't even have been able to see it."

"Do I have to split you up?" Larry said.

"Ha!" Frannie answered. "Usually it's me saying that to you and Mickey."

"Hate to break this up, but the girls are on clean up," Ben said.

Jane Ann grimaced. "I'm afraid to go in my camper after you guys have been in there."

Nancy got up and started stacking plates. "Might as well get it over with. And then can we have dessert?" She looked pointedly at the men.

"Oops. I knew we forgot something," Ben said.

Frannie let out an exaggerated sigh. "Fortunately I have an orange cake inside. It would be really good with lemon custard ice cream. Wish we had some."

"Oh! I just happen to have some in the freezer," Jane Ann said.

"They planned this," Mickey said to Ben. "I will help the girls out and take the garbage to the dumpster."

Larry and Ben rearranged the fire, adding more wood while the cleanup was in progress.

A tan Department of Natural Resources truck rolled slowly by. The ranger nodded and pulled up at the popup camper two sites down from them.

"They were having trouble with their electrical hookup," Frannie said. "Wonder if they got it fixed?" She picked up the chicken platter and a bowl to carry them in to Ferraros' coach.

When she came back out, a sheriff's car had stopped behind the ranger's truck. The sheriff and the ranger stood in the middle of the road in serious discussion. "What's going on?"

"We don't know—probably something to do with those sirens we heard earlier," Larry said.

As they watched, the sheriff reached through his car window and pulled out a plastic bag. He held it up to show the ranger, who shook his head.

Mickey passed them, looked at the bag with interest, and hurried back into the campsite. "That looks like another one of those trackable tags."

"Larry, go find out what's happening," Frannie said.

Larry put his hands up. "Why me? If you want to know, ask them yourself."

"You don't want me to snoop," Frannie said. "You were a cop so if you ask them, it will be professional interest. They *would* think I'm just a snoop."

"Like that's ever bothered you before." He got up, but hesitated.

Mickey said, "We might be able to help if it has something to do with those turtles."

Larry scoffed. "Don't encourage her." But he walked over to the two men in the road. He spoke to the sheriff and shook hands, introducing himself. The group watched as he pointed at the bag and then back at them. As he talked, he rubbed his hand over his crew cut and the sheriff nodded, asking questions. The ranger stood back, looking apprehensive. Finally the sheriff led the way over to their table.

Larry introduced each of them. "This is Sheriff Jackson and we met Ranger Stevenson earlier." He looked at Frannie. "Explain what you found out about the turtles."

Frannie had laid their turtle on the table and explained how the trackables worked.

The ranger cleared his throat and then said quietly, "I've seen a lot of people hunting for the caches in the park but don't know much about it."

"Where did you find that one?" Jane Ann asked, pointing to the bag in the sheriff's hand.

"I'm asking for your discretion because we haven't released this yet, but you may be able to help." He took a deep breath and held up the bag. "A man was found dead in the woods across the creek from the CCC Museum and not from natural causes. This was found near the body."

CHAPTER THREE

THURSDAY EVENING

"BUT WE WERE just in that area before supper, hunting a cache," Nancy said.

"And the shoe..." Frannie said. She felt a little disoriented; originally afraid when she found the shoe, relieved that it was just a shoe, and now this.

Ranger Stevenson muttered something to the sheriff and left. The sheriff sat down at the table. "Okay, I need you to walk me through this little hobby. How do you know where to look?"

Frannie got up. "Let me get my laptop and we can show you." As Frannie brought the laptop out, the setting sun seemed more ominous, the few clouds more threatening. Her stomach clenched. The thought of a man lying dead near where they had found the cache was too much to grasp.

On her laptop, she showed the sheriff the list of caches and pointed out the one where she and Mickey had found the turtle. "This metal tag attached to the plastic turtle makes it a 'trackable.' We entered the number and found out there are three more of these in different caches in the area. If you find all four, you are supposed to put them in caches farther west. They started on the East Coast and the goal is to get them to the West Coast."

The sheriff looked at the turtle Mickey and Frannie had found and then at the tag in the bag. He said, "So this tag was attached to one of these turtles?"

"Maybe," Frannie said. "Although it could have been some other item and maybe not part of this turtle thing."

"Do all of these caches have something like this in them?" the sheriff said.

Mickey broke in. "No, some have items to trade—just little trinkets—and some just have a log to sign."

"And the one you just found near the museum?" the sheriff asked.

Frannie pointed at an item in the list. "That was this one."

"But there wasn't a turtle or a tag in it?"

"No, it was too small," Jane Ann said.

"Is there any way to tell where this one came from?" He held up the plastic bag.

"We can with that number that's on the tag," Nancy said.

"But we really shouldn't tell a Muggle," Jane Ann said.

"What's a Muggle?"

"You," Frannie said. "Anyone who isn't a geocacher."

"Ladies," Larry warned. "Sheriff Jackson doesn't have time for nonsense."

Frannie shrugged and typed in the tracking number for the tag and showed the sheriff the instructions.

"It should have a turtle attached—the one called Mikey. Look at the last log. It tells who moved it last and what cache they moved it to."

She expected the sheriff to make fun of the silly game but he appeared to be concentrating on the screen. After a minute, he looked up.

"Looks like Greek to me."

"Beglar26 is an user name. That's the person who brought the turtle from the last cache to the one in the park. Chocolate is the name of the cache that he or she put it in, um—looks like five months ago—late fall," Frannie said.

"That's a cruel trick," Mickey said. The sheriff looked at him and waited.

Mickey shrugged. "The name. Cuz there wouldn't be any real chocolate in it." He noticed the sheriff's expression. "Not important."

Sheriff Jackson scratched his head. "Is there anything about these turtles that would be worth killing for? Any 'treasure' of real value connected to this?"

"There shouldn't be," Larry said. "It's just for the fun of the hunt."

Jackson frowned and turned back to Frannie.

"Can you find where that cache is, or is supposed to be?"

Frannie clicked on the link and brought up the map. After zooming in and out several times, she got it to a size that she could recognize some landmarks. "There's the museum," she said, "and the creek. So it's on the other side of the creek, almost directly across from the

27

museum. We would put these coordinates in our GPS to locate it." She went back to the details page on the cache. "According to this, it hasn't been found since the turtle was put in it. So if someone found it recently, they didn't log it online. Not yet anyway."

"That's a heavily wooded hill. I may ask you to help me with that tomorrow. So there's at least two more in the area that have these turtle things?" the sheriff said.

"Supposed to be," Ben said. "Unless someone removed them."

"What did you say about a shoe?"

"When we were searching behind the museum— down by the creek—we found a shoe. We thought..." Frannie paused, "we thought it was odd." It didn't seem prudent to mention at this time that they had turned up dead bodies on previous camping trips and had been afraid of what might be in the shoe.

"Can you show me?"

"Sure."

"Who else was with you?"

"Jane Ann and Nancy."

"Okay. I'd like you three and Mr. Shoemaker too, if you would, to come with me."

The ranger walked back up to the group. He was quite young and looked like he expected a scolding. "Excuse me, Sheriff, but Saturday and Sunday, we have that Dolomite Decathlon scheduled here as a fund-raiser for the park. Will we need to cancel?"

The sheriff didn't answer immediately. He looked at his watch. "I'll stop back after we check this out. Want to get down there before dark. Is this one of Normadean's projects?"

The ranger nodded unhappily.

Sheriff Jackson put his hand on the ranger's shoulder. "I hope we won't have to. Neither of us wants to give Normadean *that* news. But we'll talk after I get these folks back."

Between the approaching dusk and the news of the body, the trees overhanging the road seemed much more threatening. Nobody talked, each of the riders mulling over the sheriff's news. Frannie, in the back seat with the other women, also felt a little guilty of something—she didn't know what—maybe just because of the metal mesh separating them from Larry and the sheriff in the front.

As they got out of the car, Sheriff Jackson grabbed a large flashlight lantern and switched it on to guide them across the open field in the lengthening shadows. They approached the creek, and Frannie pointed out the pile of rocks where they had seen the shoe. But when they arrived, the flashlight revealed nothing.

"It was on that rock." Nancy pointed. "I poked it with my stick and it fell on the ground there by the bushes. We didn't pay any more attention to it. Or touch it."

"You said you found the 'cache' around here?" the sheriff said.

"Aim your flashlight at that little tree," Frannie said. She climbed over the rocks to get to the shrub area and grabbed the pinecone from the crotch of the tree.

"A pine cone?" the sheriff asked.

29

"It's not real." Frannie turned it over and popped the panel on the back. She showed the sheriff the tiny tube.

"Is there anything in it?"

She unscrewed the top. "Just a log—a piece of paper to sign that you found it." She watched the sheriff's face. Did he suspect them of something?

"What kind of shoe was it? What size?"

"A hiking-type shoe. Definitely an adult size, kind of a tan color" Jane Ann said.

"Where did they find the—body?" Frannie asked.

The sheriff looked at her but didn't speak at first. "In the woods across the creek," he finally said.

"Was he missing a shoe?"

"That's confidential at this point."

Frannie sighed. "Do you know who it is? Someone from the campground?"

Larry said, "Frannie…"

Sheriff Jackson considered that. "No, someone local. Okay, that's all we can do here tonight. I'll take you back to your campsite."

They trooped back to the car in silence, glancing at each other and shrugging in disbelief and confusion. Again the ride was silent.

When the sheriff pulled up to the campsite and let them out, he said, "I do appreciate your help and would like you to show me how to find that cache in the morning. Are you available?"

They all nodded and he continued. "Okay, I'll be back about 9:00." He rolled up his window and pulled away.

CHAPTER FOUR

THURSDAY NIGHT

MICKEY AND BEN sat by the fire, laughing. Ben wiped his eyes and looked up at the returning group.

"What's so funny?" Frannie said.

"Something inane, no doubt," Jane Ann said. "I'd rather not know."

"Well?" Mickey grew serious. "Spill."

Larry walked over to the cooler by his trailer, got out a beer and opened it. "Not much to tell. The girls showed him where they found the cache and a shoe, but the shoe was gone."

Mickey looked at his watch. "In just a couple of hours? That's strange." He hummed the theme from *Jaws*.

"Did he tell you any more about the victim?" Ben leaned forward to stir the fire.

"Careful," Mickey told him. "I built that teepee for Larry."

"The way it *should* be done," Larry said. "Your log cabins are okay for cooking but that is the best gathering fire."

"I think I've heard this argument before," Ben said, put his stick down, and drew back into his chair. The 'firefight' between Mickey and Larry over whether a teepee or log cabin structure was better provided endless —and sometimes exasperating—conversation for the group.

"Only a million times," Frannie said, pulling up another chair. "The older Mickey and Larry get, the more they can't remember what they've argued about and they have to rehash it all. To answer your question, Ben, the only thing he would tell us is that the guy is local. Thank goodness."

They all looked at her.

"I mean, I'm just glad it's not someone from the campground. We won't be involved."

Larry laid his hand along the back of her neck. "Dear, you are already involved. And if you weren't, you would find a way to be."

"Not true! It's always inadvertent." But she couldn't help but smile a little.

"She can't keep a straight face when she lies," Larry told the others.

A voice interrupted from the edge of the campsite. "Excuse us? Do you know what's going on?"

The couple from the popup was standing in the road with a small white, dust-mop type of dog on a leash. The woman was short, solid looking but not fat, and appeared to be in her late fifties. Soft gray-brown curls formed a halo around her face. Her husband was about the same height, but wiry. They walked closer to the campfire.

The man smiled and held out his hand to Larry, who was still standing. "Hi. Name's Darius Lumley. Saw you talking to the ranger and that sheriff earlier. Just wondered why he was around. Somethin' goin' on?"

Larry hesitated. "A man died in the park. You probably heard the sirens and chopper earlier."

"Oh, my," said the woman. "Heart attack?"

"Not exactly. They said it wasn't natural causes. That's all we know."

Darius Lumley's smile disappeared. "You're kidding."

Larry shook his head. "No."

"Wow." Darius turned to his wife. "Odee, I think we might want to sleep in the truck tonight." He said to Larry, "That's the trouble with popups; they aren't very secure."

Frannie said, "I saw your license plate—are you from Kentucky?"

"Yes, we are," the woman said.

"So is this a destination or just a stopover?" Jane Ann asked, while Nancy pulled a couple of extra lawn chairs up.

"Oh, thank you. We can just sit a minute—Peaches needs her walk." The woman sat and pulled the dog up in her lap. "I guess you could say it's a destination." She glanced at her husband as if for approval. "We bought some land in this area a couple of years ago and wanted to check it out." She hurried on. "Pretty country. This is really a beautiful park."

"It's one of our favorites," Frannie said. "I didn't catch your name..."

She smiled. "It's kind of odd. Odee." She spelled it. "My mama named me Ophelia Delilah. Can you imagine? Bless her heart, she was a wonderful woman but must have been on somethin' when she named me. So my big brother just called me by my initials and it stuck."

Frannie laughed and introduced the rest of the group.

Darius turned to Larry again. "You're saying somebody was murdered?"

"Well, we don't really know. I guess it could be a suicide, but we probably should all be a little more careful."

"That's the only reason we let Larry camp with us," Mickey said. "He's a retired cop so he's our bodyguard."

"In your dreams, Ferraro," Larry said. "If my sister hadn't been foolish enough to marry you, I probably would have done you in myself a long time ago."

Darius and Odee looked alarmed for a moment and then realized it was just a joke.

"So they were talking to you because you were a cop?" Darius asked.

"Not really. We do a little geocaching and they found something that seems to be out of a cache in the park," Larry said.

Odee nodded. "I've heard of that—looking for stuff that other people have hidden?"

"That about sums it up," Nancy said.

"How did you happen to buy land up here?" Ben asked the Lumleys.

"Through an internet land company. Iowa has such good farmland. I got a little inheritance from my dad a couple of years ago and had just gotten downsized out of my job so decided to invest in some really good land. But they haven't been able to rent it yet so we decided to come see what was going on. I'm worried that someone has ripped off my life savings," Darius said. He frowned, bushy eyebrows drawing together and face flushed.

Odee looked at her husband, concerned. She put the dog on the ground and got up. "Well, we don't even know if they've rented it or not because we can't get hold of the property manager. But we haven't gotten any money out of it. We'd better get our walk in, hon, and leave these nice folks alone."

Peaches leapt around in excitement and Chloe, on Nancy's lap, gave a low growl in her throat. Cuba barely opened one eye from her spot beneath Larry's chair. In her estimation, Peaches was too small to be noticeable.

They all said their goodbyes and watched the Lumleys stroll on down the road.

"That property thing sounds a little shaky," Ben said.

Jane Ann went to refill her wine glass. "What do you mean, Ben?"

"They bought this land two years ago and still haven't received any rent from it? Iowa farmland? And can't contact the property manager? I'd be wondering."

"You mean some kind of scam?" Nancy said.

"There're a lot of scams on the web," Larry said.

Mickey sat forward in his chair. "No way! I got an email from someone in Nigeria who wants to make me their heir if I sent them just a few thousand bucks. I'm sure it was on the up and up so I took the money out of Jane Ann's retirement fund—Oww!"

Jane Ann removed her foot from her husband's and gave him a smug grin.

Larry laughed. "She's done that since she was two. It's a wonder I can even walk."

"Seriously," Ben said, "I just read about people who post pictures of houses that they've copied off of realtors' sites and offer them for rent. People who send deposits and first month's rent arrive to find the house isn't for rent at all. Buyers pull scams too."

"I would think that would be hard," Nancy said.

"The sale doesn't have to go through for the scammer to make money. The most common practice is to send a deposit check for more than the amount requested; then ask for a refund of the extra. And the original check is no good."

"Well I hope this isn't a scam. Doesn't sound like they have money to throw around," Frannie said.

The conversation went back to the city council shenanigans for a while, until Frannie produced the orange cake and Jane Ann got the ice cream out of her freezer.

While they were dishing up, Mickey glanced down the road. "Those folks were serious. They're hauling blankets and pillows out to their Suburban."

"Can't say as I blame them," Nancy said.

Ben put down his plate and said to his wife. "We can close our beds up and just open up the couch if you want."

Ben and Nancy's camper was a hybrid—a small trailer with drop down beds on each end with cloth sides similar to those in a popup.

Nancy was conflicted. She was normally down-to-earth and practical, not easily alarmed. But the wind was picking up a little and mewling through some of the still-bare tree branches. The few other RVs, scattered throughout the campground, provided only distant, isolated pinpricks of light in the moonless night.

"It's probably silly, but maybe we should," she said. She grimaced. "I just got the bed made up."

"I'll help," Ben said.

As he and Nancy headed to their trailer, Jane Ann said, "Ben is such a good husband."

Mickey said to Larry, "I told you we shouldn't invite him."

"Yeah, yeah."

"I wonder what all is included in this decathlon thing Saturday," Frannie said, savoring the spicy cake, sweet oranges and smooth ice cream.

"Oh, I picked up a flyer when we registered." Jane Ann reached in her jacket pocket and pulled out a brochure. She spread it out on the picnic table in the light of a lantern. "I think you'll want to sign up, Frannie." She looked up and grinned. "For adults, there's a 3K and a 5K run, bike race, a cross country obstacle course through the woods, softball throw, archery, arm wrestling..."

"Okay, okay, give it a rest," Frannie said. Her lack of athleticism was as well known as her fear of heights.

"But you get a t-shirt and the proceeds all go to the park."

"I'll make a donation."

Jane Ann continued down the list. "Here at the bottom it says they need volunteers to help with the timing."

"I could do that. Are you going to enter anything?"

"I don't know. Might. I bet Nancy will."

"You guys are a lot younger than me," Frannie said, and then looked at Larry and Mickey. "Not a word from you two."

Mickey pantomimed locking his lips and throwing the key into the fire.

The Terells returned to the fire. Mickey had gotten out his guitar and was picking out a soulful tune. Jane Ann and Nancy pored over the brochure for the decathlon. Frannie vowed once again to get in better shape so that she could keep up with her sister-in-law and friends. She also knew she probably wouldn't keep that vow. Her only bow to additional exercise was collecting the plates and forks and returning them to the camper.

Finishing her glass of wine, she listened to the chatter around the fire, another favorite thing about camping. But when she glanced toward the vast darkness surrounding them, she gave an involuntary shudder.

CHAPTER FIVE

EARLY FRIDAY MORNING

THE NEXT MORNING, Frannie maneuvered down her camper steps with the dog and the coffee pot and peered up at an overcast sky. Disappointing, but at least there wasn't any rain in the forecast. And, of course, the weather forecasts were never wrong.

She had pulled a hooded sweatshirt over her pajamas and slipped into moccasins, so after plugging in the old percolator, she hooked up Cuba's leash to take the Lab on a loop around the campground. In spite of the gray skies, the temperature was bearable and, best of all, there was no wind. As she circled back past the Lumleys' site, she noticed Odee sitting by a small fire wrapped in a tattered blanket. She gripped a mug with both hands and appeared to be in deep thought.

When she heard Frannie approach, however, she looked up and her face brightened.

"Good morning," Frannie said. "How did you sleep?"

"Oh, fine—we've slept in there before and with an air mattress, it isn't bad."

Frannie nodded. "We used to tent camp and if the weather was threatening, we often slept in our SUV and used the tent for a changing room. Eventually we decided we were too old to sleep on the ground at all and that's when we bought our trailer."

Odee sighed. "We'd like to trade up—doesn't have to be anything fancy—but until we figure out this land thing, we can't do much else. I wish we'd never made that investment."

Frannie hesitated. "Do you think it's—on the up and up?" She hesitated to say 'a scam.'

"I don't know. Darius was sure it's fine, but he's been having second thoughts lately." She shrugged. "We're going to the courthouse today to check the records. I hope we'll find out something one way or the other."

"Well, good luck," Frannie said, nudging Cuba up from her version of 'downward dog.' "Let's go."

When she got back, Larry was up and working on a fire. She poured a mug of coffee and plopped in her chair.

"Morning exercise?" he said.

"Hey, better than nothing." She looked at her watch. "What time did the sheriff say he was coming back?"

"About 9:00."

"I need to shower so how about if we do a simple breakfast? There's cereal and I'll get the toaster out. I got some rhubarb jam at that place we stopped on our way up yesterday."

"Fine."

When Frannie returned from the shower house, Larry was at the table with his cereal and toast, arguing with Mickey over the Cubs and the Cardinals. Nancy and Jane Ann were also having breakfast.

"Where's Ben?" Frannie said as she toweled off her hair.

"He went for a run."

"He's going to enter the 5K tomorrow," Nancy said.

"Show off," Frannie said. "You're all show offs."

Larry got up, his spat with Mickey forgotten as quickly as it had probably started.

"Go ahead and get your breakfast and I'll enter the coordinates for that cache that the sheriff wants to look for in the Garmin. What was the name of it?"

"Chocolate," Mickey said. "How could you forget that? You have a mind like a steel mesh."

"Don't start again," Jane Ann told her husband. "Give us a break."

Frannie laughed and followed Larry into their trailer.

WHEN THE SHERIFF arrived, he suggested Larry and Frannie trail him in their truck to parking area C accessing the woods. On the way, Frannie told Larry about her conversation with Odee that morning.

"What do you think? Do you think it could be a scam?"

"Sounds pretty fishy, doesn't it? Did she say where this land is?"

"No."

They parked and walked over to the sheriff. Frannie switched on the Garmin and waited for it to locate a satellite. She pointed into the woods in a slightly uphill direction. The sheriff motioned for her to lead, he followed and Larry trailed behind.

41

As they started into the woods, Frannie said over her shoulder, "Can you tell us yet who the victim was?"

Sheriff Jackson grumbled. "It'll be on the news today, I guess. It was Frank Leslie, a local farmer. His place adjoins the park."

"Did he have any enemies or do you think it was random?" She tripped over a root and caught herself on a tree.

"Frannie, you'd better concentrate on where you're going," came Larry's voice from the back.

The sheriff laughed. "Is she always like this?"

"I'm afraid so."

The woods had that early spring smell and Frannie spotted May apples and Dutchman's Britches poking up through a thick carpet of last year's leaves. Clumps of trillium provided bright spots of white deep in the woods. A bit of orange caught her eye downhill from their track.

"Are those flags?"

"They're planning a cross country run and obstacle course as part of the fundraiser this weekend. They're going to have to move the route though, because of the murder."

"Wow—they're going to try and *run* through these woods?" Frannie could barely stay upright on the steep slope.

"Some people are crazy."

"So did Frank Leslie have any enemies that you know of?" Frannie persisted.

The sheriff was panting a little as they climbed the hill at a slant. "Well—there's been talk of him selling that land for an ethanol plant. A lot of folks aren't too happy about that for various reasons."

"How 'not too happy' are they? Enough for murder?" Frannie said.

He shrugged. "Who knows? We don't have much homicide around here. I'm sure it's the same where you live. But in cases I've read about, it seems in the right circumstances almost anything might be cause for murder."

"Does he have a family?" Larry said, causing Frannie to look back at him and almost stumble again. Usually he didn't like her asking questions and tried to stay out of these situations himself.

"Wife died a few years ago." The sheriff stopped, took off his hat, and wiped his brow. "Kids are grown— two girls and a boy. None of them live around here— actually one of the girls is in some institution for mental problems, I think. Zach, the son, is coming in this morning and I don't know about the other daughter. She, Tracy, was once engaged to Ranger Stevenson, but they broke it off."

"The ranger did or the girl?" Frannie asked.

"I really don't know." He motioned Frannie to continue.

She watched the screen on the Garmin. "Okay. We should be about twenty feet away from the cache." She stepped over a fallen tree and picked her way through the brush. Finally she stopped.

"It's not very accurate when it gets this close." She looked up at the sheriff and made a circle with her arm. "It should be in this area."

Jackson looked around at the logs, trees and tangled shrubs and put his hands on his hips. "Needle in a haystack."

"Not as bad as you think," Frannie said, opening a folded paper. "There's a clue that says 'Look at your feet' so it's probably down low. It says it's 'small' so probably about the size of a piece of bread. Usually a plastic container with a tight lid."

Larry started slowly moving around the area, lifting vines and brush to peer underneath, but the sheriff still didn't move.

"What if it's buried?"

"Against the rules," Larry said.

"Maybe since the name is 'chocolate,' it's dark brown. Sometimes the name means something; sometimes it doesn't," Frannie said, searching the area across from Larry. She caught a glimpse of yellow out of the corner of her eye, downhill from where they searched. She turned and saw a flutter of yellow ribbon mostly hidden by the trees. Crime scene tape.

"Is that where—?" she said to the sheriff.

He nodded. "That's why I want to know where that turtle came from."

Frannie prodded a pile of leaves and sticks with her foot. A sharp pain through her sock and the toe of her lightweight tennis shoe caused a clutch of fear. Snake, she thought, and jerked her foot back. There was no movement. She gingerly lifted the pile with a dead branch, prepared to bolt. A gleam of dull metal emerged.

"How was the victim killed?" she asked the sheriff.

"He was stabbed," he said. "Now that's all the information I'm going to give you."

"Did you find the weapon?"

"Mrs. Shoemaker, this is an investigation and the details—"

Frannie interrupted. "Because if you didn't, maybe I just did." She pointed at the pile.

The sheriff walked over to the pile, pulled out a handkerchief, and gingerly picked up a knife. He held it up. The handle was partially rotted and the blade was rusty.

"Looks like it's been there a long time," Frannie said, disappointed.

"It does," the sheriff said, "but we'll test it anyway." He dropped it into a bag that he produced out of another pocket.

"It poked my foot. As rusty as it is, I hope it didn't break the skin." She examined the toe of her sock for signs of blood.

"I bet your tetanus shot isn't up to date," Larry said, as he moved to the downhill side of the clearing. He pushed aside clumps of leaves and brush and peeked under fallen trees.

Frannie continued to move uphill, thinking that Larry was probably right. She couldn't even remember her last tetanus booster. A hollow under a fallen log seemed promising but yielded only wet leaves. Meanwhile, the

45

sheriff made a half-hearted attempt to look like he was helping.

"Got it!" Larry reached over and picked up a plastic sandwich box. "Looks like it was just dropped—not hidden."

Frannie and the sheriff joined him on either side as he opened it.

"Empty," Frannie said.

"It's could be from somebody's lunch," the sheriff suggested.

"Could be," Larry agreed. "There should at least be a log in it, and a pencil or pen, but there's nothing."

Frannie looked around. "What if the person was interrupted? Either as a witness to the murder or the perp—"

The sheriff raised his eyebrows and couldn't hold back a little smile. "The perp?"

"She watches a lot of crime shows," Larry muttered.

Frannie continued staring closely at the ground. A spot of blue peeking from under some leaves caught her eye. She bent down and pulled out a pencil stub. "I bet this came out of the cache. Look for a scrap of paper. If the finder signed it, maybe we can identify them."

"We?" Larry said with a grin.

"The sheriff can," Frannie said.

They had been searching for about ten minutes when Sheriff Jackson said, "Is this it?" He held up a strip of adding machine paper, torn at each end. "There's dates and initials and gibberish on it."

Frannie examined it. "That's part of it. But see, the last date is last summer, so there must be more that was torn off. That turtle should be around somewhere, too."

"Do people ever not sign the log?" the sheriff asked.

"I don't know any reason they wouldn't, if they're geocachers. The website keeps track of how many you find so that's part of the challenge," Larry said. "I guess sometimes people who are not geocachers might find one and take things out of it or move it altogether."

"Muggles?" the sheriff said.

"Muggles," said Larry.

They continued to search a widening area with no luck. The sheriff moved down toward the yellow crime scene tape, looking in that area. Finally he looked at his watch. "Well, I've got an interview to do, but at least now I know what to look for. Thanks for you help." He motioned them to go ahead of him, politely indicating that they wouldn't be hanging around this area.

"And you have a weapon—the knife," Frannie reminded him.

"Maybe," he said.

CHAPTER SIX

LATE FRIDAY MORNING

ONCE IN THE truck, Frannie took off her shoe and sock to examine her toe. The skin wasn't broken, just red. Another life-threatening disease averted.

"Emergency room?" Larry asked.

"Not this time." She put her sock and shoe back on.

"You should write a camping guide complete with nearby medical facilities." He grinned at her.

"Very funny."

When they arrived back at their campsite, Mickey and Ben were playing cards at the picnic table.

"Where're Jane Ann and Nancy?" Frannie asked.

"They went for a run. I'm surprised you didn't pass them somewhere," Ben said.

"It's a big park," Frannie said. "Boy, they're really serious about this thing tomorrow." She felt a little left out but knew it was her own fault.

"Did you find anything?" Mickey said.

Larry described what they had found and also had learned about the victim.

"Sounds like a local deal," Mickey said. "There've been more objections raised in recent years to ethanol."

Larry feigned disbelief. "What, did they cover that on Saturday cartoons?"

"Hush," Frannie said. "*And*, he forgot to mention, I found a knife."

"It's probably the weapon if the murder occurred fifteen or twenty years ago," Larry said.

Frannie ignored him. "So if we assume that tag came out of that cache, there's two more we need to find or Mickey's going to have to scale the cliff to put the first one back."

"Yeah, but—won't they keep the second one for evidence?" Ben said.

"Probably but I think we could get a duplicate—or explain on the trackables site that it was moved from 'Chocolate' to 'County Evidence Lockup.'"

Mickey laughed. "That's appropriate since the turtles are fighting crime on their way across America—although in this case, Mikey wasn't very effective. Why was that cache named 'Chocolate' anyway?"

"No idea," Frannie said. "But while we're waiting for the Olympic hopefuls to return, I'll get my laptop and we can pick out a couple of targets for today."

THEY WERE STUDYING the list of caches when Nancy and Jane Ann returned. At least, Frannie thought, it gave her the chance to see her two friends looking tacky for once. And sweaty. And out of breath. They both gathered supplies and took off for the shower house but at a slower pace.

While they were gone, Frannie and the men organized their hunt.

"Here's one that's a large size so it could have a turtle in it," Frannie said. "Looks like it's near the amphitheater."

"And this one is in the picnic shelter area." Ben pointed at the screen. "It says small so it would work, too."

"Okay—teams," said Mickey. "How about I'll go with Ben and Nancy and you guys can take Jane Ann."

"That's a treat," Larry said. "I get my wife *and* my sister?" Frannie slugged him in the arm.

They managed to agree, loaded the coordinates in their Garmins, and copied down the clues.

"This would be easier if you would bring a printer along, Frannie," Mickey said.

"Do you want me to slug you too?"

The other women returned and were brought up to date on the plan. Within fifteen minutes, both groups were loaded in the pickups and headed out.

Frannie noticed when they passed the Lumleys' spot that the SUV was gone. Probably out checking on their land. She hoped for their sake they would find good news.

Once again they had to leave the park and take the county road to the north entrance. Frannie was turned in her seat to talk to Jane Ann when Larry said, "Whoa! Wonder what's going on up there?"

Ahead, on the normally deserted gravel road, cars and pickups lined the ditch and several people gathered by a farm lane, some hoisting signs. Frannie could make out danger symbols on several of the signs and one read 'Save our water; save our land.'

Larry slowed as they neared the group. "This must be where they want to build the ethanol plant—the place owned by the dead guy."

"There's the sheriff's car in the lane," Frannie said.

They edged slowly by the group and Frannie sat up straight. "Larry! Up by the house! That looks like the Lumleys' Suburban! Do you suppose this is the land they bought? Or thought they bought?"

Larry leaned over the steering wheel and peered up the lane. "Methinks the plot thickens."

Most of the protesters drew back to let them pass. One young man, with an incongruous beard and buzz cut, moved threateningly toward the truck, forcing Larry to slow even more. As they drew abreast, he smacked the front of the truck with the flat of his sign. Sheriff Jackson jumped out of his car and shouted.

"Mark Masters!"

The young man turned and glowered at the sheriff. Jackson waved the Shoemakers on and headed for the kid.

Frannie and Jane Ann craned their necks back as they continued down the road until Larry turned back into the park. Frannie related what they had learned from the sheriff that morning about the victim.

"So you didn't find the whole log?" Jane Ann said.

"Nope."

"We could go back there later and search some more."

Larry sighed. "Jane Ann, don't encourage her. It's a *crime scene.*"

"Not there, it's not," Frannie said.

The road wound down into the valley of the river that had formed the park and then leveled out along the river as it meandered between the dolomite cliffs. Larry pulled into a small parking area by a sign that said 'Amphitheater.'

He turned to Frannie. "I've never been up to this place. What does the GPS say?"

"A quarter of a mile, straight up that hill. Seems like there's an awful lot of climbing for these caches."

At least there were wide steps built into the hill with landscape timbers.

"This is a multi-cache, did you notice that?" Jane Ann said as they climbed.

"Huh," Fannie said. If she said any more, her shortness of breath would become apparent. She *really* needed to work out more.

They reached the amphitheater, which was built into a natural bowl with simple seating, also of heavy timbers. At the bottom of the bowl was a small wooden platform with a white screen supported on two heavy posts behind the platform.

They stood looking down at the stage while Frannie checked her handheld GPS. She pointed toward the stage. "That way, 60 feet."

"The name of this one is 'Stage Fright' so I guess that's a big clue," Larry said, leading the way down the steps.

The area around the stage had been cleared so there wasn't brush or trees to hide anything in. Jane Ann walked around the stage, stooping to peer underneath, while Frannie searched the posts and parts of the screen she could reach.

"Aha!" Larry said, standing by an electrical post. He held up a tiny metal container with his thumb and forefinger.

"Where was it?" Frannie said.

"It's one of those magnetic ones, just stuck to the post. The grass around the bottom hid it."

He unscrewed the lid and pulled out a minuscule roll of paper. Since this was a multi-cache, this container would only tell them where to go next. "Okay," he said to Frannie, "ready to input these coordinates?"

"Just a minute." Frannie changed screens and opened a new waypoint. "Okay, shoot."

Larry read the numbers and letters slowly as she typed them in. When he finished, he replaced the roll in the container and reattached it to the post. Frannie turned on the new waypoint. She led the way into the woods away from the stage. The GPS led them to the base of a small cliff.

"Oh, no," Frannie said. "I'm not climbing any more cliffs."

Larry took the Garmin from her and peered at the screen. "It should be right nearby."

They circled the area and it was Jane Ann who spotted something in the hollow end of a fallen tree. She pulled out some dead leaves and pieces of bark that had been used to partially conceal a plastic paint container with a screw-on lid. The whole thing was covered with camouflage duct tape.

She unscrewed the lid and peered in. "A real treasure trove," she said and pulled out a plastic robot, some stickers and a key chain. She continued pulling out various small toys, a patch and other tiny items. "Here's the log," she said, and pulled out a pocket notebook.

"Anything to write with?" Larry asked. She handed him a fat green crayon and he grimaced.

"Frannie, do you have a pen or pencil?"

She rummaged in her pockets and produced a pen.

"I've never seen so much stuff in one cache," Jane Ann said, still extracting items. "Here it is!" She held up a small green figure with a tag attached.

"All right!" Frannie said. "Only one to go. What's the last date on there, Larry? Maybe the same person found it that found the one by the murder scene."

Larry shook his head. "It's last fall. Besides, if someone found it recently, why wouldn't they have taken the turtle?" Larry signed the log and put the notebook back.

"Oh, right." Frannie pocketed her pen.

They trudged back through the trees and to the top of the amphitheater; then back down the stairs to the truck. The crowd was still gathered at the farm lane when they passed. A compact van with the logo of a local TV station had shown up, but they didn't see any sign of the Lumleys' light blue SUV or the Mark Masters character who had accosted them earlier. The crowd seemed more subdued and had pulled back to the side of the road.

When they pulled in at their campsite, Ben's truck wasn't back yet. Frannie brought her laptop back out to the picnic table and logged their find plus the discovery of the trackable. She was just finishing when Odee Lumley walked up.

Odee looked overwhelmed and was twisting a lock of hair around a finger.

"Can you help us?"

"What?" Frannie blurted, surprised, but then realized how rude she sounded.

Jane Ann sat her coffee mug on the table, more collected and sympathetic as usual. "What's happened?"

Odee clasped her hands to stop her fidgeting. "That man—the man they found—he owned the land we bought. Or thought we bought. Or—we went to the farm —we recognized the house from the pictures. His son was there and said his dad never sold that land. And the sheriff started asking questions—and—I think he suspects us of, you know—having something to do with his death."

CHAPTER SEVEN
FRIDAY NOON

FRANNIE CLOSED HER laptop and slid down the bench to make room. "Odee, you'd better sit down. Would you like some coffee or a glass of water or something?"

"No—yes, I mean, a glass of water sounds good, if it's not too much bother."

Jane Ann got up. "I'll get it."

"So the farm you thought you were buying...?" Frannie said.

"Is right on the outside of the park," Odee said, gratefully accepting the water and taking a big gulp. "But there're people protesting there now because the sheriff said that the guy was thinking of selling the land for an ethanol plant."

"He told us that, too," Frannie said. "What happened to the management company that was supposed to be handling it for you?"

Odee scoffed. "Good question. No one there ever heard of them. I think our money's gone." She hiccupped a little and started to cry.

Frannie leaned over and hugged her.

Jane Ann said, "What makes you think the sheriff suspects you of the death?"

Odee took a deep breath and got herself under control. "He just asked a lot of questions about how long we had been here, where we were the last couple of days, like that."

"But he didn't give you a warning or offer you a lawyer?" Frannie said.

Larry had walked over to the table and stood listening.

Odee shook her head and looked up at Larry. "Since you were a cop, can you help us?"

Larry held up his hands and backed up a step. "Whoa. I'm retired, Odee. I don't have any business interfering with this investigation."

She looked defeated and shrugged her shoulders helplessly. "Well, do you think we should get a lawyer? We don't know anyone around here."

"I don't think that's necessary at this point." Larry rubbed his hand over his crewcut. "It sounds like there were several issues involved and probably other more viable suspects."

Odee's face relaxed slightly.

Ben's yellow pickup passed the site and pulled in at the Terells' trailer. Doors slammed and the three were laughing as they came around the end of Shoemakers' trailer.

Mickey pumped a fist in the air and yelled, "Found it!"

"Another turtle?" Jane Ann asked.

He deflated a little. "No, but we found the cache."

"How about you guys?" Nancy stopped by the utility table to refill her mug from the old percolator.

"Found ours too," Larry said smugly. "It was a multi-cache and even so," he looked at his watch, "we've been back for hours. Oh, and what was that other thing that was in it?" He looked at Frannie. She held up the turtle with the tag.

Mickey quickly forgot his disappointment. "Cool! Which one is that?"

"This one's Raph. And the one with the body was Mikey."

"So there's only one more? We should be able to find that in the next three days."

Nancy noticed Odee sitting at the table. "How are you this morning?"

Frannie shook her head at Nancy, but apparently Odee didn't want to talk about it any more. "I'm fine. Is that one of those treasure things you're talking about?"

Nancy laughed. "There's not much treasure involved, unfortunately, but yes, we just found one of the caches and Larry and Frannie found another one this morning."

"I helped," Jane Ann said.

"What's for lunch?" Mickey said. "I'm starved."

"Whatever you find," his wife answered.

He tromped into their coach.

Odee got up. "I'd better be going. It's time for our lunch, too."

By the time Frannie had fixed sandwiches for herself and Larry and returned to the picnic table, Mickey was sitting with a heaping plate. She examined it. "What on earth do you have there?"

Mickey rotated the plate to display his selections. "Half a leftover chicken breast, some grapefruit sections, a hot dog, a peanut butter brownie, and a piece of French bread with some leftover smoked salmon from the other night. Why?"

"Never mind."

Nancy came over with a fresh green salad festooned with pea pods, mushrooms, and oranges.

"That looks lovely," Frannie said.

"Mmmm," Nancy said, her mouth full. She finished chewing and swallowed. "When we were leaving the shelter area, they were setting up the registration for the decathlon. I thought I'd go back after lunch and register for the 5K."

"I'll go too," Jane Ann said.

"Me too," Frannie said.

Larry looked at her in surprise.

"I'm going to volunteer to help." She added, "Jane Ann said they are looking for people."

"I didn't say anything," Larry said.

"You didn't need to."

"I'll be inside."

Frannie was clearing her dishes when the ranger walked by. "Hello!" she called out. "Sounds like it's going to be a big weekend."

He nodded and sauntered over. His uniform was crisp and his belt loaded with paraphernalia. Apparently he was fairly new and very proud of all the trappings.

He tried to look weighed down by responsibility and sighed. "I appreciate all that the Friends of the Park do, but this is not going to be the best time to have a lot of extra people in the park."

"I guess you knew the victim? Or at least his daughter?"

His face changed for a fraction of a second. "Um, yeah. We dated for a while but it didn't work out. I know you shouldn't speak ill of the dead, but Frank Leslie was not a pleasant man. Or a happy one."

Frannie thought he looked like he wanted to talk. "What do you mean, not happy?"

"He was cruel, and the kids refused to come home any more."

"Such a waste," Frannie said. "I can't imagine having that kind of relationship with my kids."

"Yeah. He's the reason Tracy and I broke up."

"I'm so sorry. That must have been very hard for you."

"He—he said he'd cut her off without a cent if she married me."

"Maybe you're better off, then, if the money was that important to her," Frannie said softly.

Now he was angry. "It wasn't the money. She hoped if we split, her dad would—warm up to her again. But it never happened. Why are you so interested, anyway?" It was as if he suddenly regretted confiding in her.

She put her hand to her forehead. "I'm sorry—I thought it was a personal loss. I was going to offer you condolences."

Stevenson straightened and his face returned to the bland newbie. "Thank you, but I don't think it was anyone's loss." He touched his hat, Old West style. She expected him to say "Ma'am" in farewell, but he just turned and walked away.

NANCY RETURNED FROM her camper and the women climbed in Ben and Nancy's truck.

"Isn't Ben going to register?" Jane Ann asked.

"He's going to ride his bike down later."

"Show off," Jane Ann said.

"You're all show offs," Frannie said.

Jane Ann turned and looked at Frannie in the back seat. "Well, good. If none of the men are going, after we register, we can go look for the rest of that log."

"What log?" Nancy said, pulling onto the campground road.

Frannie explained what they had found with the sheriff that morning.

"Ahhh," Nancy said. "Definitely. We have a much better chance of success without the men."

"At least, less badgering without Larry." Frannie then brought Nancy up to date with Odee's situation and Ranger Stevenson's revelations.

Nancy shook her head. "What a mess." She pulled in the parking area near two large picnic shelters.

A large, professional-looking banner hung from the eaves of the one nearest the road. Several people scurried around the area directed by a man in tight black pants and a pink windbreaker. He had his back to the road and turned as the women approached the shelter. And Frannie realized her mistake.

The person was the type of woman described as 'big-boned' and a perfect inverted triangle. Broad shoulders narrowed to a thick waist, flat butt, and the skinniest legs Frannie thought she had ever seen. The woman was heavily made up, which contrasted with her short, mannish haircut. She started to greet them, but was distracted by Ranger Stevenson, who was stacking some forms on the table.

"No, Sid, those go at this end of the table," she said sharply.

"I think this might be Normadean," Frannie whispered.

CHAPTER EIGHT

EARLY FRIDAY AFTERNOON

"LADIES!" THE WOMAN called out. "Welcome! Are you here to register?"

"We are," Nancy said.

The woman gave them a fleeting smile and returned to business. "Right over here—start at this end of the table and Paula will help you. There're forms and schedules there. Be sure you fill out your tee shirt size correctly because we can't send them back, you know."

"I'm not here to register, but your flyer said you need volunteers," Frannie said.

The woman put her hands on her hips and thrust out her considerable chest. Sure enough, a badge on her jacket said 'Normadean Paddlefield.'

Frannie was glad she didn't have to fill *that* in on any forms.

"Do we ever! The sheriff is asking me to post people all along the 5K route because Frank Leslie went and got himself killed in the park. Now where, I ask you, am I going to find that many people this late?"

63

Frannie assumed the question was rhetorical and at the same time wondered if Frank Leslie knew what an inconvenience his death had been. "So, what can I do?"

Normadean produced a clipboard with a list of names in small, tight printing.

"Give me your name, and spell it please. Are you local or staying in the park? Better give me your cell number, too — you do have a cell phone, I hope?"

Frannie was relieved she could answer affirmatively, because she expected a lecture was in store if she couldn't. She spelled her name and gave her phone number. There were other questions, too — her license plate number, CPR and first aid training, and the names of any other similar events that she had volunteered for. They were certainly picky for being desperate.

"Now, I'll need all the volunteers here by 8:30 sharp tomorrow for your assignments. The run starts at 9:00 and believe me, that doesn't give me much time to get people to their assigned places. Better make it 8:00."

Frannie nodded so much that she felt like a bobble-head doll.

"Do you know anyone else who can help?"

Frannie looked at Jane Ann. "Possibly our husbands. We'll ask them."

"Don't ask them, honey — tell them. I need everyone I can get." She checked on Paula's progress, apparently making sure she was on the right track.

Jane Ann had her lips pursed and her cheeks puffed out, suppressing a giggle.

Frannie didn't dare look her in the eye. "Okay, we'll see what we can do."

Nancy finished her registration and they walked back to the truck. Once they were back inside, Nancy let out a peal of laughter.

"No wonder the sheriff and the ranger are afraid of her!" Frannie said.

"For sure," Jane Ann agreed.

NANCY FOLLOWED FRANNIE'S directions to parking area C.

"Do you have your GPS with you?" Nancy said.

"No, but I think I can find the site. There's a bunch of crime scene tape just down the hill, where they found that guy."

Easier said than done. They angled farther uphill than they should have and finally Frannie said, "I think we've gone too far." The woods on all sides of them had a sameness that was disorienting. The only variation was the slope toward the lake. "We're almost to the top of the of the ridge. Let's head downhill from here a ways and then back toward the truck."

Going downhill was less strenuous than going up but it was harder to get footing. Finally, Jane Ann pointed downhill and to the right. "There's the crime scene tape."

They angled toward it until Frannie chose a spot just uphill from it as being the right place. They spread out to examine every inch of the ground in about a twenty-foot-circle. There were a few gum wrappers and a crushed Styrofoam cup, but no paper log.

Frannie realized she was too close to the crime scene, so turned to head back uphill. She ducked as a robin with twigs in its beak swooped past and landed by a nest on a nearby tree branch. Among the twigs and grass of the small nest was a small scrap of white.

Frannie moved closer and waited for the robin to leave again. He (or she) cocked his head at her and left for more building materials. Frannie climbed on a nearby stump and stood on her toes to reach the nest.

"Frannie! What are you doing?" Jane Ann called.

Startled, Frannie caught herself on the tree trunk and reached up and gently tugged at the piece of paper. Some of the twigs and grass drifted to the ground but she managed to get the paper loose without upsetting the entire nest.

"Frannie!" Now Jane Ann was directly behind Frannie, who tumbled backwards off the stump knocking Jane Ann to the ground.

Jane Ann swore, Frannie screamed and Nancy turned and covered her mouth.

"*What* are you doing?"

Frannie rolled off of Jane Ann and lay on the ground, a groan becoming laughter. She turned her head and said, "Does she think there's an answer to that question?"

Jane Ann gasped and snorted, sending both into more giggles.

Frannie raised her arm straight up, brandishing the scrap of paper. "Got it!"

"And it was so easy," Nancy said, grabbing the slip from Frannie's hand.

Jane Ann got up, grunting, and gave Frannie a hand up. They brushed off their jeans and each other's back while Nancy picked twigs out of their hair.

"That robin could use these for her nest. Save her a lot of time," Frannie said, holding a fistful of grass.

"So, what are you going to do with this?" Nancy said. "Turn it over to the sheriff, I assume?"

"I guess." Frannie unrolled the scrap to read it.

"Frannie, we'll have to," Jane Ann said. "Not only because it's evidence, but the only way to find out who the last finder was is for the authorities to request that information from the website."

"I'm not so sure," Frannie looked up and grinned. "We need to find a phone book."

"Why?" Jane Ann peered over her shoulder.

"The user name is 'bmyers' — not difficult to check out. The date is smudged, though."

"Oh, dear," Nancy said.

"Actually, we don't even need a phone book. We'll just go back and do a search on line. And if we see the sheriff along the way, we'll give it to him."

"Maybe we should make *sure* we find the sheriff along the way." Nancy started to lead them back toward the parking lot.

"You're right. I need to stay out of this. If we don't see the sheriff on the way back, we'll find him after we check in with the guys. We've been gone quite a while." Frannie became lost in thought as they bounced and jounced back to the campground.

"Frannie?" She got the feeling it wasn't the first time Jane Ann had called her name.

"Huh?"

"What is your job tomorrow for the race?"

"Well, I don't really know. Normadean said she needs people all along the race route because of the murder. So I guess we just stand there."

"And what are you supposed to do if the murderer decides to take out a couple of runners?"

"Not sure. I probably should have taken that martial arts class at the school last winter."

"You can take your Ninja turtle along for protection," Nancy said. "Seriously, Larry's not going to let you do that. What is Normadean thinking?"

"To be fair, I think it was the sheriff's idea—not hers. And if I can get Larry and Mickey to help, we'll be fine. Even better, maybe this will lead to an arrest and we won't have to worry." Frannie held up the slip of paper.

"Ha!" Jane Ann said.

When they got back to their campsite, Frannie told Larry about her volunteer responsibilities.

"Is that where you've been this whole time?"

"Pretty much," Frannie said, turning to go into the trailer.

"So what's this?" He pulled a leaf from the back of her hair.

"Oh."

Larry just raised his eyebrows and waited, the offending leaf still in the air.

Frannie held up the slip of paper. "We found this."

Larry folded his arms and looked skeptical. "Found? At the race registration?"

"My fault," Jane Ann said. "It was my suggestion."

Larry frowned at his sister. "It's a crime scene."

"Not where we were," Jane Ann said.

"Larry, this was stuck in a bird's nest. It's the end of the log. We plan to give it to the sheriff." Frannie didn't add that she also thought they might be able to identify the last signer themselves. Maybe the person's identity would help clear Odee and her husband.

"How upstanding of you both." Larry was not happy.

"Do you want to go with us to supervise?" Frannie said.

Ignoring her sarcasm, Larry said, "Yes. I'll call him first."

The sheriff was back at the Leslie farm. There were a few protesters still there but the lane was open. When they pulled up, Sheriff Jackson was standing by a big white Hummer in what looked like a heavy discussion with a heavy-set, ruddy-complexioned man who was definitely not dressed for farm work. A younger woman, similar coloring but more relaxed, leaned against the Hummer. The sheriff excused himself and walked toward them. Larry, Frannie and Jane Ann got out of the truck but waited for him there. Larry leaned against the fender and nodded to Frannie.

"Um, Sheriff, we did some more searching at that spot where we found the cache this morning and found this stuck in a bird's nest." She held out the scrap of paper.

The sheriff took it with two fingers and raised one eyebrow. "I assume there's not much chance of fingerprints now."

Frannie felt her face flush. Between being married to a cop for years and her favorite TV shows, she should have thought of that.

"Sorry," she mumbled.

The sheriff examined the paper. "So what does this mean?"

"That's the user name of the last person who signed the log." She pointed without touching the paper, like she could undo some of the damage. "Maybe the website will give you their information."

"Thanks for your help — I think." He looked at Larry.

Apparently a little 'guys' club' thing, Frannie thought in disgust.

"We *were* trying to help," Jane Ann said. "We've done a lot of geocaching." She opened the truck door to get back in.

"Hey! I've got better things to do than wait around while you exchange notes." It was the ruddy man, who had come up behind the sheriff.

The sheriff sighed and backed up to admit the man to the group. "This is Zach Leslie, son of the...deceased." He turned to Leslie. "These people found a clue that may be helpful in finding your dad's murderer."

The man snorted. "Clues schmooze. You've got plenty of suspects. You need to get this wrapped up so I can get on with business."

Larry opened the driver's door. "We'll get out of your way, Sheriff."

The sheriff nodded. "I'll talk to you later about this."

As they drove back down the lane, Jane Ann said, "Sometimes grief affects some people strangely, doesn't it?"

"Seems to me he should be one of the suspects," Frannie said.

Larry shook his head but said nothing.

At the lane entrance, most of the protesters stood stoically, holding their signs and watching the pickup. A couple shook their fists.

"Apparently, we are part of the threat," Larry said.

Frannie decided to change the subject. "The lady at the race registration—the famous Normadean—wanted to know if you and Mickey would also volunteer to help at the race tomorrow."

"What would we have to do?"

"Use your bodies to shield us runners from any marauding murderers in the woods," Jane Ann piped up from the back seat.

"What?"

"They want volunteers stationed all along the route as a safety measure," Frannie explained.

"And what do you plan to do if said murderer comes bursting out of the woods?" Larry asked Frannie.

"Good question," Frannie said. "But I wasn't going to argue with Normadean. Once you meet her, you'll know why."

CHAPTER NINE
LATE FRIDAY AFTERNOON

WHEN THEY RETURNED to the campsite, Larry and Jane Ann joined the others at the table to fill them in on the latest. Frannie went into her camper to fix a glass of iced tea and find some snacks. When she spotted her laptop on the dinette, she remembered her plan to research 'bmyers' in northeast Iowa. Possibly Myers was too common a name to narrow down but it was worth a try.

She first checked the white pages. Of course, if the person didn't have a landline, and many people didn't anymore, that search would be fruitless. She narrowed it down to the nearest town, Blueberry Hill. There were seven Myerses listed, two with first names beginning with 'B.' She wrote them down. Then another possibility crossed her mind. The geocacher could be someone from the campground. She could check the registration cards on the posts. Some campgrounds even posted a list of the campers in reserved spots at the entrance.

She picked up her tea and a bag of chips and returned to the group.

"What were you doing?" Larry asked. He was never nosy unless he suspected her of being involved in what should be police work.

"Oh, just a little picking up—you know."

From his look, he didn't believe her; they both kept things pretty orderly in the camper. But he let it drop.

Frannie hooked up Cuba's leash. "Anyone else want to go for a walk? I feel like I've spent most of the day in a truck."

"Getting leaves in your hair," Larry said, but she ignored him.

"I'll go," Nancy said. "Just let me get Chloe's leash."

They started toward the south end of the campground, which was starting to fill up with weekend arrivals. Frannie tried to remember which campers had been there the previous night but she checked the registration posts of all just in case—surreptitiously, of course, so Nancy wouldn't notice.

"What are you looking for?" Nancy asked.

So much for that. "Just wondered if there might be a Myers camping here."

"Ohhh, right. But maybe it's a local person."

"Maybe, but it could just as easily be a camper."

"True."

They continued around the loop, keeping their eyes peeled. A couple of A-frame popup campers, looking like hard-sided tents, caused them to stop and comment. Frannie pointed out a red and silver teardrop—a small trailer named for its shape.

"Well that was fruitless," Nancy said as they neared their own campsite.

"Not really." Frannie grinned at her. "Site 37 is a Myers."

"Why didn't you say something?"

"Because he was sitting at his picnic table. It was that cute red and silver teardrop."

"Ohhh. Good call."

The rest of their group was intently watching a new arrival attempting to park a large fifth-wheel in a small spot across the road. Frannie and Nancy promptly joined this popular form of campground entertainment.

A harried-looking woman stood by the pad, alternating 'c'mon' motions with both hands held up, palms forward, in an unmistakable 'Stop!' signal.

"No, Bob, left, left!" she called, pushing her hair back from her face. "Stop! You're going to hit the post!"

Brakes screeched and the truck door slammed after the driver descended to check for himself. He returned to the driver's seat and pulled back out. His second attempt avoided the site post, but not the overhanging branches of a tall pine growing along side the pad. The fingernails-on-blackboard sound of the branches dragging on top of the camper made them all cringe.

"Oh, man," Ben said. "That looks like a new unit, too."

Bob got out again and rummaged in one of the storage compartments, all the while keeping up a heated argument with the woman.

"What's he doing?" Nancy said.

Bob emerged from the compartment and held up a tool.

"Looks like a pruner — can't tell for sure," Larry said.

Their questions were answered when Bob went to the back of the camper where the outside ladder was and soon appeared on the roof. He cut back several branches of the pine and threw them to the ground.

Jane Ann sat forward in her chair. "Can he do that?"

"He just did," Frannie said.

Bob came around from behind the camper, picked up the branches, threw them to the side, and got back in the truck.

"I'm guessing the ranger will have a talk with him," Larry said.

The driver continued his backing. The woman glanced their way and quickly went back to her signals.

"At least she has the grace to look embar—" A loud crunch interrupted Nancy's comment.

Ben bolted out of his chair and went to the road so he could see the other side of the camper. He came back suppressing a smirk. "He hit the power post." He held his hand up at a slight angle. "Not too bad, but I don't imagine it did his camper any good."

"It's pretty funny as long as it isn't one of us," Mickey said.

"You think it's funny as long as it isn't *you*," Larry said. "You think it's *especially* funny if it's one of us."

"He'll have to explain those branches to the ranger when he comes to check the power post," Nancy said.

"Speak of the devil," Frannie said, pointing at the tan DNR truck just rounding the corner.

They watched as the man flagged down the truck and explained his dilemma to the ranger. The ranger went to look at the post and as he walked back, stopped to examine the pine boughs. He then raised his eyes to the tree above the camper roof and looked pointedly at the man still standing by the road.

The man rubbed his head and looked down at the road, then seemed to launch into an explanation. Since they couldn't hear the conversation, they lost interest and returned to a discussion of the murder.

Mickey said to Frannie, "Larry says the victim's son is really torn up about his dad's death."

"Yeah, he's torn up about it interrupting his business."

The Lumleys' Suburban passed on the way back to their site. Darius waved absently.

"Wonder if they found out any more about their land," Jane Ann said. "They're having a rough time, especially being under suspicion and all."

"I like Zach Leslie better as a suspect," Frannie said.

"That's because you like him less as a person," Larry said.

"Of course. Obviously you don't know much about crime investigations."

Across the road, the ranger left and Bob pulled his truck and camper out on the road and proceeded to maneuver it into the campsite farther from the power post and the pine tree. The woman sat at the bare picnic table, arms crossed and anger on her face.

"It might not be a fun evening in their camper," Nancy said. "I hope there isn't another murder."

"Speaking of which, here comes the sheriff," Ben said.

At the sight of the official car, Bob, who was working on his setup, looked up and his eyes grew wide. He didn't relax until the sheriff was headed toward Frannie's group.

"Okay," the sheriff said, "first I need to know if you want to press charges against the kid who whacked your truck this morning."

"I don't think so," Larry said. "Kind of a hot head, huh?"

Jackson shook his head. "He's been one of the organizers of this protest since it started. He's fully convinced about the risks of an ethanol plant but he doesn't have much common sense or tact when it comes to getting something done."

"There's a lot of people like that—everywhere," Frannie said. "What is his main objection?"

Jackson shrugged. "Who knows? I think he's active in a couple of environmental groups that object to taking land out of conserved acres to grow corn. The focus on corn cuts down on crop rotation so they add more chemicals. But some people are upset about what it will cost the county to maintain roads with so many heavy trucks. And there's the water issue too."

"Now," he said, looking at the three women, "explain to me how you 'happened' to be in the area and found that slip of paper."

Nancy took the lead and gave a concise report of events.

"So you deliberately went looking for it?" The sheriff's voice had changed and it was obvious his patience was wearing thin.

"Sheriff, we aren't trying to interfere," Frannie said, ignoring her husband rolling his eyes. "We've done quite a bit of geocaching and knew what we were looking for. You asked for our help earlier."

"You knew what you were looking for? Maybe you knew what you were looking for because you were there when the murder occurred? And even if you weren't, by handling the paper, you may have destroyed any useful fingerprints."

"What? We weren't anywhere near there. We were right here, having supper," Frannie said.

The sheriff cocked his head and gave a sly smile. "This happened before supper. And you told me that you women were hunting one of those caches then. Maybe you were on the other side of the creek. I haven't ruled you people out."

He nodded, turned, got in his car and drove away.

"Well," Larry said.

Frannie ignored him. "You know, if there was a witness, they may not have signed the log before they saw Frank Leslie."

"True," said Nancy, "so 'bmyers' might be the previous finder."

"Frannie," Larry said. "We need to talk." He headed to the trailer.

"Hoo boy," Frannie said and trudged behind him. Jane Ann high-fived her as she passed.

When they got inside, Frannie said, "Larry, you are turning into a real male chauvinist. It's embarrassing that you treat me like an idiot around the sheriff and our friends. What's gotten into you?"

Larry crossed his arms. "This has nothing to do with gender or intelligence. It has to do with your lack of experience and the law. I should have put my foot down the other times—you need to keep out of it. Now he suspects us of being connected to the case."

She felt her face flush. "Larry, we helped solve those cases."

"They would have done it without us. You do not have the expertise to avoid compromising evidence. That's why watching *CSI* doesn't qualify as training for a law enforcement career."

"I understand that, of course. But I'm not sure those cases would have been solved as quickly without us. I don't see what it hurts to talk about it."

"It doesn't but you're going beyond that. Damaging evidence and possibly endangering yourself."

"I know and I'm sorry about the evidence. But it wasn't intentional and the end of the log might not have been found if Jane Ann and I hadn't looked." She sighed. "I was just trying to help. I'm going to the restroom."

She left and headed back around the trailer, away from the group. Tears stung her eyes, which was always her physical response to anger. She walked to the shower house and splashed water on her face. After a couple of deep breaths, she returned outside and looked around a little.

Most of the sites in this loop were occupied. Several were younger families who probably wanted to be as close to the shower house as possible. A twenty-something couple was working on a pop-up. The woman, with long brown hair that she constantly flipped back, was getting a pile of blankets and pillows out of the back of their car. She looked up and smiled at Frannie. "Hi."

"Hello. Here for the weekend?"

"Um, yeah." She chewed her lip. "First time. Can you tell?"

Frannie laughed. "No. But you'll get the hang of it."

"Oh, I'm not worried about that. Just—" she looked over at the woods, "—what about animals and stuff?"

"Animals?" Frannie said. "You mean like raccoons? That's mostly what's here."

"Or snakes? Bears?" the girl said, and giggled nervously.

"Not too many bears that I've ever heard of. A few snakes on the trails but not usually in the campground."

"It's just that I've always lived in Chicago. Those woods look pretty scary."

"Compared to Chicago? I can't believe that!" Frannie said.

"No, really, it doesn't bother me at all to walk at night or take the bus or El in the city, but *that* is scary." She indicated the woods again and shook her head. "Silly, isn't it?" She went back to unloading her car.

"Well, good luck," Frannie said and continued around the campground away from her campsite. She could walk off some of her anger. Most people were out, making supper preparations.

As she passed site #37, a youngish man with a crewcut had the back hatch of the teardrop open to the outdoor kitchen and was pulling a grill out of one of the storage compartments. He looked up and said, "Hi! Nice afternoon."

"Not bad," Frannie said. "At least it isn't raining."

He laughed. "And in Iowa in the spring, we have to be happy with that, don't we?"

"For sure. That's a great camper, by the way."

"Thanks. We love it. It's usually just my son and I so it fits our needs perfectly," he said. "I come here a lot but my son couldn't join me this time, unfortunately. He loves it. Beautiful park, isn't it?"

"One of our favorites," Frannie said. "We do a lot of geocaching and there's quite a few around here." She watched his face carefully as she said this.

He seemed a little disconcerted, but she couldn't be sure. "Geocaching?"

"Yeah, people hide stuff—actually all over the world —and list the coordinates on the Geocaching website. Then you use a GPS to find them. Or at least try."

"Sounds fun," he said and went back to his grill. "Better get this out and fired up if I'm going to have any supper." He smiled.

She walked on. Either he found her description of geocaching extremely uninteresting or he had something to hide.

WHEN SHE RETURNED, Odee and Darius Lumley had joined the group and Larry was deep in conversation with them. He glanced up as Frannie returned and then resumed his chat. She had calmed down but not enough to forgive him. And she hated it when he was right. She pulled a chair up next Jane Ann and told her about the young woman who was more afraid of camping than the streets of Chicago.

CHAPTER TEN

FRIDAY NIGHT

SUPPER WAS ONE of their typical potlucks. Each couple brought their own meat to grill and a side dish to share. At the table, Jane Ann asked Larry what was happening with the Lumleys.

He gave Frannie a look. Frannie figured he thought she had put Jane Ann up to asking. She fidgeted in her seat but he responded.

"A management company was supposed to be collecting rent for them and apparently doesn't exist. They also went to the county courthouse this afternoon and Frank Leslie is still the owner of record. I'm afraid they've been duped."

"Oh, wow," Nancy said. "What a shame."

Larry nodded. "I told them to report it to the feds—probably the Interstate Commerce Commission—but I think their money is gone for good. At least they won't sink any more money into it. They've been suspicious for a while but were afraid to quit paying in case it was on the up and up."

"How are they taking it?" Ben said.

"Better than I thought they would. They seem to be somewhat relieved to have a definite answer. Odee especially."

"Can they sue?" Nancy said.

"You can always sue, but you can't necessarily win. Who would they sue?" Mickey asked.

"Well, I guess I mean Frank Leslie or his estate."

"They'd have to show that he was involved in the scam," Larry said.

As they cleaned up the table afterwards, Mickey said, "I was talking to a guy in the next row and he says an old buddy of mine, Gary Krukow, is playing at a local bar tonight—The Wander Inn. I played with Gary a little in college. I think we ought to 'wander in,' as it were." He grinned as he scooped the leftover potatoes into an old sour cream tub.

"What does he play?" Nancy asked.

"Guitar and a little banjo. Mostly folk stuff; some blues."

"I'm game," Ben said and the rest agreed.

THE WANDER INN was a typical small-town tavern. It took Frannie's eyes a moment to adjust to the dark interior. Beer signs above the bar shed a little light. Faux-country sconces with red-checkered shades above each table tried bravely to do their part.

They took an empty table and Ben went to the bar for a pitcher of beer. There was a small, low stage in the back corner across from the bar. No one was there at the moment, but three guitars were propped on stands around the microphone, patiently waiting. Loud voices clattered greetings, insults and good-natured arguments.

"Mickey Ferraro, you old dog!" A very short man approached their table, holding out his hand.

Mickey stood, grabbed the hand with his right and slapped the man on the shoulder with his left. His eyes lit up and he broke into a broad smile. "Gary! I was just telling these guys about the good old days. You remember my wife Jane Ann?" He introduced the rest of the group.

Gary greeted everyone and thanked them for coming, brushing back his thick mane of grey-blonde hair. "Gotta go but we'll visit during the next break." He returned to the stage and picked up one of the guitars. He began the set with several folk tunes from the Sixties.

The group hummed along and tapped toes to the familiar melodies from their younger days. "I love the music from this era," Frannie said. "At least there was a message."

Larry leaned over to Mickey and said, "I can see why you were friends. He's the only guy I've ever met who's shorter than you."

Mickey laughed. "You got it!"

Gary set down the acoustic guitar he'd been playing and picked up a banjo from a table behind him. He leaned into the mike.

"Folks, I once tried to teach a guy to play this, but he's a slow learner. So on one number, I asked him to fake it. It would have fooled everyone if he had stopped strumming when the song ended." The crowd laughed and Gary said, "Ferraro, get up here!"

Mickey made a weak show of protest, but stood up and jogged to the stage.

"That's the fastest I've ever seen him move," Ben said.

"That's the fastest *any* of us have seen him move," Jane Ann said.

Gary and Mickey conferred and Mickey picked up the acoustic guitar. After a few mis-starts, nudges, and laughter, they broke into *This Land is Your Land*. The crowd clapped, stomped and sang along. Next they sang *Tom Dooley*.

Frannie leaned back in her chair. The mood changed with the somber song but there was a feeling of being totally comfortable, surrounded by good friends and good music. She didn't even resist when Larry put his arm across her shoulders.

She looked around the crowded room. Some people were into the music, others greeted friends or ordered at the bar, and a young woman delivered baskets of onion rings and other goodies. A group of men came in the front door, laughing and talking loudly. One looked familiar; then Frannie realized it was Zach Leslie. He was in the center of the group and the others vied for his attention, pulling his sleeve or tapping his shoulder to point out others in the bar. He was certainly hiding his grief well.

The men took a table nearby, shifted chairs around, changed places, and passed pitchers of beer. Their antics blocked the view of the stage but they seemed oblivious to the performance or anyone around them.

A dark-haired man whistled a waitress over to complain about something. Gary frowned slightly but upped his volume to compensate for the distraction. Finally the group settled a little as Gary and Mickey finished up *Mighty Day* and Mickey took a little bow before returning to his seat.

"*That* wasn't easy," he said before taking a sip of his beer.

"You mean competing with those rowdies?" Ben asked.

Mickey looked surprised. "No. We're used to that. I meant only two of us doing a Chad Mitchell Trio song."

"The guy with the reddish hair is Zach Leslie, the son of the murder victim," Frannie said.

Mickey stared at the group. "So is this a wake?"

"Right," said Nancy.

A tall, scrawny guy stopped by the table of men. He was probably only a little older than the men at the table, but his weathered face and bent body made him appear much older.

"You guys still think you rule the roost around here, dontcha? You're wrong. And one of these days we're gonna find out what you did with my little brother and you won't be such hotshots then," he growled.

Momentary shock crossed the faces of the men.

Zach snarled, "Maybe you should think about what your little brother did to my little sister and shut your face."

The others snickered and shared knowing looks. The scrawny guy appeared angry but shook his head and continued to the bar.

Mickey leaned over the table. "What was that about?"

The scrawny man stood at the bar and took a long drink from a bottle of beer. He stared at himself in the mirror and was joined a moment later by a large woman in a royal blue velour sweat suit.

Nancy poked Frannie. "Isn't that—?"

"Normadean Paddlefield? I believe so."

"Wow. If that guy sics her on that table of bullies, they'll know what for."

Frannie chuckled. "For sure." But seeing Normadean jogged her memory. "Larry and Mickey, that's Normadean over there at the bar. Are you guys willing to help at the race tomorrow?"

"Sure," said Mickey. "What do we have to do?"

"Mostly stand along the route." She looked pointedly at Larry.

He shrugged. "Okay."

"I'll go tell her." Frannie got up, avoiding Larry's gaze.

When she got to the bar, Normadean and the scrawny guy had their heads together. Frannie hung back behind them, hesitant to interrupt. The woman put her large, mannish hand on his shoulder. "They will solve it sometime, Ed, they will. No one can keep a secret in this town forever. And somebody knows."

"Zach Leslie knows," Ed said.

"Maybe," Normadean said, "but if you get yourself in trouble, it won't bring Brian back. And I believe it will be solved. You need to be patient. I think something will happen soon. Frank thought he could bury the evidence but it will come out eventually."

Ed looked at her with a puzzled expression and noticed Frannie.

"Excuse me?" Frannie said. The woman turned, questioning at first but then recognized Frannie and smiled.

"One of my volunteers, right?" She clapped her hands. "You're still going to help, I hope!"

Frannie smiled. "Definitely. And I think I have a couple more willing volunteers for you." Willing, if not enthusiastic.

"Oh, good." Normadean hefted a giant red leather bag onto the bar. Frannie would have guessed that it would take at least eight months to find anything in it, but Normadean immediately produced a lime green notebook. "Watch this," she said to Ed, nodding toward the purse. She led Frannie to a nearby empty table and plopped down. "Now. Give me their names."

Frannie did along with the answers to all of the other questions she had fielded herself that afternoon.

"Thank you," Normadean said, slapping her notebook closed. "Remember you need to be there at 8:00 sharp. And I could use more people Sunday, too for the obstacle course."

"Sure, I'll think about it." Frannie paused. "I couldn't help but see your friend's confrontation with that loud group of guys. Is everything okay?"

Normadean lowered her voice. "His brother Brian was murdered years ago. He's always blamed Zach and his friends, but the case was never solved."

"Oh, how awful. What a difficult situation. Sorry to bother you, but I will see you tomorrow." Frannie got up and Normadean went back to the bar.

Back at her own table, Gary was taking a break and regaling the group with reminiscences about his college days and performing with Mickey. Frannie half-listened as she considered this latest bit of local history. Was it just coincidence that Frank Leslie had been killed and his son may have been involved in an earlier murder?

"A penny for your thoughts," Jane Ann said.

"Oh...nothing. Been a long day, I guess."

"We should get back and get to bed. Besides the decathlon tomorrow, we also have a turtle to find."

"And a murderer," Frannie said and then glanced quickly at Larry to see if he had heard her. Luckily, he was laughing at Mickey and Gary.

Jane Ann squinted at her in the dim light. "Do you know something you haven't shared?"

"I know lots of stuff I don't share," Frannie grinned.

"I mean about the..." she glanced at Larry, "...you know."

"We should have a secret code," Frannie said. "Need to hit the restroom?"

"Sure."

THE WOMEN'S RESTROOM was small but clean with old wood stalls and trim. Frannie washed her hands and dried them on a paper towel. "That scrawny guy's name is Ed and his brother was murdered several years ago. He thinks Zach and his friends were responsible."

"Wow!" Jane Ann pulled the scrunchy out of her hair, brushed it, and pulled it back into a smooth ponytail.

Frannie leaned against the entrance door and watched with envy—she always thought her sister-in-law resembled Grace Kelly.

"Did Normadean think there was anything to it?" Jane Ann asked.

"She wouldn't say. She told Ed it would be solved one day and urged him to stay out of trouble, but he didn't seem to be buying it. Actually, she said she thought something would come out soon. She seemed to think that Frank Leslie knew something about it, too."

"Sounds like there must be a connection," Jane Ann said, as she slipped her brush back into her bag. "Why else would she think that?"

"That's what I think—oof!" Frannie jumped as someone pushed on the door, almost knocking her over.

"Oh, I'm sorry." Normadean poked her head in the door.

"No, my fault," Frannie said. "I shouldn't have been leaning on it."

"Well, I'm glad to catch you like this, anyway. I don't know if you know any of the local people but it's best not to bring up Brian's murder." Normadean swung the red

To Cache a Killer

purse up on the vanity and deftly extracted a tube of lipstick. "Most people feel pretty strongly about it one way or the other and it won't make you any friends." She applied the bluish-red color, pursed her lips, and dropped the tube back in the bag.

"We don't know anyone in town," Frannie said. "We're just weekend campers."

"Good," Normadean said, and charged back out the door.

"Close your mouth, Jane Ann," Frannie said.

"Did she just say 'Mind your own business'?"

"Larry probably paid her to."

"And how does she find anything in that purse?" Jane Ann said.

"Amazing, isn't it?" Frannie led the way back toward their table.

Jane Ann lowered her voice. "Anyway, it seems pretty suspicious that Zach Leslie might have been a suspect in a murder years ago and now his dad has been murdered."

"Exactly."

Frannie glanced over at the bar and saw Normadean now deep in conversation with Mark Masters, the protester who attacked their truck. She guessed that wasn't too surprising; if Normadean was a big supporter of the park, she probably wasn't in favor of the ethanol plant either.

92

CHAPTER ELEVEN

EARLY SATURDAY MORNING

THE SUN'S RAYS were just beginning to angle through the trees at the campground when Frannie poured her first mug of coffee and settled in her lawn chair. Cuba had collapsed at the side of the chair after their short walk.

Frannie considered her situation. Larry was right, much as she hated to admit it. She needed to stay out of this investigation. She hoped the Lumleys were not involved and she didn't know any of the other suspects. But a little thinking about it wouldn't hurt, would it?

Like, what was the connection between Normadean and Ed and his brother Brian? It seemed pretty odd that Normadean was in the bar last night—not a place Frannie would have expected to see her. Of course, she really knew nothing about the woman. And that knife—any connection to the murdered man? It could have been dropped there years before with no sinister purpose whatsoever.

Then there was the mystery geocacher. Everything pointed to some kind of interruption. She had never seen a cache left like that. She sighed and picked up the mystery she'd been reading, but couldn't get into it.

As the sun rose higher, others began to stir around the campground. At least it looked like this would be a brighter day than the day before, and that lifted her mood. Nancy walked around the end of the trailer, carrying her own steaming mug.

"Morning!"

"It is and looks like it's going to be a nice one," Frannie said.

Nancy pulled a chair up next to her.

"So, this morning the race and then we have another turtle to find." Nancy ran one hand through her short, spiky hair. "Heavy day." She smiled.

"For sure. I don't know how we do it. What time is it? I forgot to put my watch on."

"6:30."

"I should be thinking about some breakfast," Frannie said. "Normadean ordered us to be there by 8:00 this morning."

"That reminds me. What were you and Jane Ann conferring about in the ladies' last night? I saw Normadean follow you in a couple minutes later—like she was looking for you."

Frannie nodded and explained what Normadean said about Ed and Brian. "Apparently she regretted the confidence almost immediately. So she came in to warn us to keep our mouths shut."

"No kidding?"

"She did."

"I was surprised to even see her there," Nancy said. "In the bar, I mean."

"Me too. I figured her for a stalwart member of the Temperance Union."

"So—both deaths have a connection to Zach Leslie. What do you think of that, Detective?"

Frannie shook her head. "I'm done playing detective. Larry's right. One of these days I'll do something that really screws up an investigation. I've been lucky so far."

"But now the sheriff suspects us. We can always just speculate, can't we?"

Frannie grinned. "I don't see why not. But right now I'd better have some breakfast and get dressed. And I need to roll Larry out."

She mixed herself a breakfast shake with a banana, yogurt and some frozen strawberries in her mini blender.

Larry came out of the bedroom, shrugging into a pullover.

"Hey," he said.

"Hey, yourself. Larry—" She stopped and looked up at him.

He raised his eyebrows but put one arm around her. "Yes?"

She took a deep breath. "You're right. I really screwed up. I'm sorry."

He clutched his chest. "Not sure I can survive this—this shock."

"Oh quit it. You've been hanging around Mickey too much."

He straightened and reached for a coffee mug in the cupboard. "That much is true. I just worry about you—

and how your actions will affect the investigation. So. What time do we have to be there?"

"8:00. I'm gonna get dressed and I'll be ready."

THE REST OF the group had gathered at the picnic table. She picked up her travel mug of coffee and as an afterthought, grabbed Larry's extra windbreaker off the hook. Jane Ann, Nancy, and Ben were doing stretches.

"This is part of the ritual, right?" Frannie said to Mickey.

"Oh, yeah," Mickey said. "They do all of this stuff so they'll look tough. I'm not fooled."

"Blah, blah, blah," Jane Ann said.

A CARNIVAL ATMOSPHERE pervaded the registration area, and Normadean was in her element, making the D-Day invasion look like amateur stuff. People milled around the shelter in bright running shorts with numbers pinned to the backs of their t-shirts or tank tops. Frannie led Larry and Mickey to a corner where Normadean, towering above people around her anyway, read names from a clipboard and waved one arm high over her head directing them to different groups.

She spotted Frannie and pointed her pencil at her. "Frannie, right?"

Frannie nodded.

"Over there by the man in the lime green shirt," Normadean yelled. "Did you bring your friends?"

Frannie supposed they were more than friends but nodded again anyway.

"Larry?" Normadean asked.

Larry raised his hand.

"You're with Wilma's group. Lady with the blue hair and red windbreaker." She pointed her pencil in the general direction. She assigned Mickey to still another group.

Larry muttered as they walked toward their groups. "You arranged this so I couldn't keep an eye on you."

"Not true. I imagine since you two agreed so late, she used you to fill in."

She didn't wait for his answer but found the man in the lime green shirt and gave him her name.

He checked off a few more names of new arrivals. One was a woman named Kristine Jackson. Perhaps related to the sheriff, Frannie thought.

A shadow caused Lime Shirt to glance up. "Looks like we're losing the sun," he said.

Frannie looked up. Sure enough, most of the blue had disappeared behind racing gray clouds. The wind had picked up too, and she pulled her jacket on and close around her body. Might not be a pleasant day for a race after all.

"The race course goes from here out along the road and back into the park to the CCC Museum," Lime Shirt was saying. "Our group has the road section. There's a small parking area by the entrance so if we take several vehicles we can leave them there."

"What do we have to do, exactly?" someone asked.

"Exactly nothing. We'll just space ourselves out along the road and stand there. There will be several deputies joining us. Everyone have your phones?"

They all began talking at once. Lime Shirt held up his hands. "Folks! Don't misunderstand me. This section is a public road. There will be roadblocks at each entrance and residents have been notified of this. We're just an added safety net." He leaned over and started pulling safety orange vests out of a box. "Everyone needs to wear one of these, and we have enough people that you won't be alone. Appreciate your cooperation."

FRANNIE CAUGHT UP with the woman named Kristine Jackson. "Could I catch a ride with you? My husband's got the truck and he's in another group."

"Sure." The woman turned and smiled. "Are you staying in the campground?"

"Yes, we are. I'm Frannie Shoemaker."

"Kristine Jackson. My husband's the sheriff and Normadean told me if Del wanted all these people out here, I'd better be one of them."

"And nobody argues with Normadean," Frannie said.

Kristine laughed. "That's the truth." She noticed Frannie's windbreaker. "Are you a cop?"

Frannie glanced down at the Perfection Falls Police emblem. "No, my husband was — retired now. I was a junior high teacher."

"Kind of the same thing," Kristine said with a smile.

"For sure."

When they arrived at the parking lot and gathered again, Lime Shirt, now with an orange vest, directed them out along the gravel road. Frannie followed Kristine while she shrugged into her vest. They ended up near the lane to Frank Leslie's farm. No protesters today due to the roadblock.

"Did you grow up around here, Kristine?"

"Oh, yes. I'm a lifer. Del and I were high school sweethearts. That old story." She smiled. "Why?"

Frannie told her about the incident with Zach and his friends the night before in the bar. "Since you're from here, what's Normadean's connection to these people? Anything?"

"She's a cousin to Ed and Brian and was pretty much raised by their parents, her uncle Claude and aunt Betty. Her own parents were worthless. Her mom was a heavy drinker and her dad would disappear for weeks at a time. And after Brian's death, Betty committed suicide. There's a lot of baggage there."

"Why do she and Ed think Zach and his friends killed Brian? Did they have a motive?" Frannie asked.

"There were rumors at the time about Brian and Zach's youngest sister, Lea."

"Rumors?"

"That he raped her. But they had dated for a while before that and she wouldn't file charges."

Frannie shivered. It wasn't just the wind, although that seemed to be getting colder.

"Your husband said one daughter is institutionalized. Is that why?"

Kristine shrugged. "I don't know that much about it. But it's a small town and everybody has a theory. She was a pretty nervous child and I heard there was a suicide attempt before she dated Brian. So I really don't know."

She stopped and looked at Frannie more closely. "Are you the people that helped Del with this 'geocaching' thing?"

"Yeah. Yesterday we found that knife. But it looked like it had been there for years."

"Oh." Kristine said. "Yeah."

CHAPTER TWELVE
LATE SATURDAY MORNING

IT WAS OBVIOUS that Kristine didn't want to talk about the knife, so Frannie changed the subject. "Normadean seems like the type that has her finger in every pie around town."

Kristine nodded. "I know. Right? She does a lot of good work—I'll give her that. But she's a little hard to take at times. We should space out a little more here."

"My husband would say I'm usually too spaced out."

Kristine laughed and Frannie moved closer to the next person about twenty feet down the line. She looked down the road in the direction the runners would approach. No sign of anyone yet.

The clouds were thickening. She gazed across the road at the Leslie farm. If Zach and his friends were involved in the killing of Brian Murray, did he also kill his own father? It seemed logical but also stupid. As she looked across the road and down the lane at the Leslie farm, she could see the white Hummer. Apparently Zach was staying there.

Some cheering from the end of the line drew her attention back to the race. The first runners were coming into view. She stamped her feet and thrust her hands in her pockets. This was supposed to be spring.

She applauded as the first runners passed. They obviously weren't cold. She really needed to get serious about more exercise. She spotted Ben toward the end of the first group and shouted and whistled. Runners were coming steadily now. Nancy appeared and waved, but she didn't see Jane Ann yet.

The flow of runners could be described by a bell curve. First a few front runners and the number increasing as the middle of the group passed. At that point, her decision not to participate seemed wiser. In that crowd, she surely would have stepped on someone's heel or tripped and gone sprawling in the gravel. Because of the crowd, she didn't see the white Hummer approaching the road until it reached the end of the lane and stopped.

Zach Leslie jumped out of the truck and slammed the door. He was not a happy camper. Actually, he was far too well dressed to be mistaken for any kind of camper.

He stood at the side of the road, hands on hips, watching the runners in disgust. Then he charged into the fray, crossing the road toward Frannie. People dodged and halted, throwing him dirty looks that bounced right off his crisp red windbreaker and khakis.

Frannie instinctively backed up as the juggernaut neared.

"I gotta get out of here," he shouted, waving his arm. "You need to hold these people off while I do."

"Me?" Frannie said stupidly.

"I don't care who does it, but somebody has to." By now he breathed in Frannie's face.

"Zach, what's the problem?"

To Frannie's relief, Kristine had hurried to her side.

"This is a public road, not your private race track, and I have a right to use it, Kris. You'd better get your husband on the horn now." His voice was now low and menacing.

"I'm sorry but we notified all of the residents about this," Kristine began but Zach cut her short.

"Well, I'm not a resident any more, am I? Not of this one horse town, thank God. Bunch of nosey hypocrites. I bet you're too busy standing around gossiping to get me out of here." He glared from Kristine to Frannie.

Frannie backed up another step.

"I have business appointments and I'm driving out of here. Call Del," he said. The threat was not subtle.

One of the deputies stationed along the road came up and heard Zach's demands.

Kristine tossed her head back. "Maybe you're not a resident but you still win the prize as the town bully. I don't need to call Del."

The deputy stepped forward. "Calm down, Mr. Leslie. There's no need for this. We will arrange to get the runners to one side and you can drive out to the north. Slowly and carefully."

"I want to go south."

"Sorry. To the north will be shorter and require less disruption of the race. It's your only option." He turned and walked to the north talking to each of the volunteers until he got to Lime Shirt, who had remained where the runners came out of the park onto the road.

Frannie watched him go, but kept one eye on the angry man. He scoffed, shook his head, and crossed the road in the same manner as before, forcing runners to dodge around him. As the deputy returned, the volunteers moved carefully through the runners to funnel them into the lane on the park side of the road.

The deputy then crossed the road and motioned to Zach to follow as he walked in front of Zach's Hummer, leading him the whole way past the runners. Brave man.

When the Hummer disappeared, Kristine shook her head. "What a jerk!"

The runners were thinning out so Frannie said, "Do you think he's enough of a jerk to have murdered that boy?"

Kristine stared in the distance. "I guess I think he's probably capable. But evidence?" She shrugged and went back to her post.

Frannie returned to watching the runners. She still hadn't seen Jane Ann and hoped that didn't mean she'd had an accident. There were just a few stragglers now — people whose faces looked like hers probably would if she was running. Finally, Normadean came charging up onto the road in a golf cart.

"That's the last," she shouted as she passed. "Thank you all for your help!"

Frannie and Kristine walked back to the parking lot.

"Well, at least everyone's still alive. Normadean should be happy," Frannie said.

"I'm not sure I've ever seen her 'happy.' Pleased maybe, but really happy?" Kristine shook her head. "She's really tense this weekend between the murder and this decathlon."

Frannie pursed her lips. "My husband is adamant that I stay out of this but I can't help thinking about it. One of the guys in the campground is under suspicion and, you know, I found that knife. And there seems to be a connection to a geocacher."

"Maybe," Kristine said, unlocking her car. "Things like this don't happen in a town like this. And now there's so many suspects."

"I know. And I decided this morning that Larry's right. But it's just such a puzzle. Right now, though, I'm worried about my sister-in-law. She was running today but I didn't see her. Hope she didn't trip or something."

"Things got kind of confusing when we had to move everyone so His Highness could get out."

"Yeah, she might have passed then."

They drove back to the registration area and Frannie sat down at a picnic table to wait for Larry and Mickey. Kristine talked to a young man working on paperwork and checking names off. She returned to sit by Frannie.

"I don't want to give Zach Leslie the benefit of the doubt but there are also a number of very vocal people around town who were upset about the possibility of Frank selling his farm for an ethanol plant."

"I heard that," Frannie said. "We saw the protesters yesterday. And one even hit our truck with his sign.

Young guy named Mark Masters, I think?" She looked questioningly at Kristine.

"Yeah, he's one of the hotheads. I could easily see him losing it with Frank and offing him."

"Offing him?" Frannie said. "And my husband thinks I watch too much TV."

"I hear you. Mine, too."

"Do you know if that Masters guy has been questioned?"

Kristine shook her head. "I don't know but I would guess so."

"Was Zach even in town the night of the murder? He obviously doesn't live here."

"On the news this morning they said he claims he was in Chicago. But Normadean says she saw lights in the house Thursday night *after* Frank was murdered."

"Sounds like that kind of weakens his alibi," Frannie said.

"Sort of but everyone knows how much Normadean hates Zach. Tomorrow morning, she's got a run through the woods scheduled. If this isn't solved by then, there could be more problems."

Ben's truck pulled up with Mickey driving. He waved at Frannie and laid on the horn.

"Just like a high school date," Frannie said.

"Is that your husband?" Kristine said.

"No, that's my brother-in-law. I'd better run or he'll leave me."

JANE ANN SPRAWLED in the passenger seat looking very tired, but Frannie still felt washed with relief. Mickey got out to let Frannie climb in back.

"I missed seeing you," Frannie said. "Did you finish?"

Jane Ann nodded, too tired to speak.

"Larry got done first in his area so he took Ben and Nancy back to camp," Mickey said over his shoulder.

Jane Ann leaned her head back against the seat. "I wasn't in shape for this," she finally said. "Ben and Nancy run all of the time."

"Well, you did it," Frannie said. "I think that's great."

They rode almost in silence—Mickey hummed along with the radio—back to the campground. When they arrived, Mickey got Jane Ann a sweatshirt and she collapsed in a lawn chair. Ben and Nancy looked far too perky.

Finally Jane Ann recovered enough to ask "Where were you stationed, Frannie?"

"On the road."

"Well, what was going on there? When I came by, they were pushing everyone to one side?"

"So that's how I missed you." Frannie went on to explain about Zach Leslie's demands.

"That guy is scary," she finished. "I wouldn't be surprised if he killed his father."

"I'm going to fix a sandwich and then watch golf," Larry said.

"'Watch golf' is Larry-speak for nap," Mickey said.

"I could use something to eat, too," Frannie said, and followed her husband to their trailer.

"Wait, wait!" Mickey said. "What time are we going to search for the other turtle?"

"2:00. Meet back here," said Nancy.

CHAPTER THIRTEEN
EARLY SATURDAY AFTERNOON

INSIDE, FRANNIE FELT welcomed by the cozy trailer and realized how cold she had been in the sharp wind. She got a can of chicken gumbo soup out of the cupboard while Larry made himself a ham and cheese sandwich.

"Larry, I know you're right about staying out of this. But I rode to our station with the sheriff's wife."

He frowned. "That was convenient."

Frannie couldn't resist a smile. "It was, actually. We were both alone and she is a very pleasant person. Anyway, she said Brian and Ed are cousins to Normadean."

Larry took his sandwich to his recliner and clicked on the TV with the remote. "Brian and Ed who?"

They hadn't really talked since the incident in the bar the night before.

"Remember the guy who stopped at Zach Leslie's table last night and accused them of doing something with his brother?"

"Yeah."

"His name is Ed and his brother's name was Brian and he was murdered several years ago. The case was never solved. And there were rumors that he had assaulted the girl he was dating—Zach Leslie's youngest sister."

"Hmmm." He was getting interested. Or his mouth was full.

"Normadean was talking to Ed at the bar when I went to tell her you and Mickey would help. I overheard her tell Ed that she thought the truth would come out soon."

Frannie took her bowl of soup over to the dinette.

Larry put his sandwich back on his plate and muted the TV.

"As long as you are so persistent in talking about this—and we are *just* talking—what about Darius Lumley?" Larry said.

"What about him? He never even met Frank Leslie."

"Yes, he did."

"What? How do you know that? Don't look so smug."

"I talked to him this morning when you were showering. He let it slip that he talked to Frank Thursday afternoon. Frank insisted he had never put his property for sale on the Internet."

"Does the sheriff know that?"

"Not yet. I haven't had time to find him."

"Oh, Larry, surely Darius didn't do it. He seems like such a mild-mannered person,"

"There have been lots of mild-mannered murderers." He turned back to the TV and turned the sound back up.

Frannie continued to eat her soup and stared out the window. She had no logical reason for not suspecting

Darius. And it was odd that Darius hadn't mentioned Thursday night that he had met the owner of the land he was trying to buy. She wondered if even Odee knew that.

She finished her lunch and took the bowl to the sink. Then she curled up on the couch with her book. The stress of the morning and the biting wind had taken more out of her than she realized and she was soon asleep.

It SEEMED LIKE only minutes later that Larry shook her gently.

"Hey. Do you want to take part in the turtle hunt?"

It took a minute to orient herself. "Yeah." She sat up and got her bearings. She stretched. "I think I could have slept all afternoon."

"You don't have to go."

"Wouldn't miss it. For one thing, I'd never hear the end of it from Mickey."

"Well," Larry said, grabbing a jacket, "If it isn't that, it would be something else."

"True," Frannie picked up her laptop and GPS. "But I really want to be in on finding that fourth turtle." She followed him out the door.

The group had gathered around the picnic table. Mickey looked like he was going to make some crack about them being late.

"Zip it, Ferraro," Frannie said as she set the laptop on the table. She looked at Ben, Nancy, and Jane Ann. "How are you guys doing? You look pretty good."

"Fine," Jane Ann said. "Much better."

111

"Enough pleasantries," Mickey said. "Let's see that list of caches."

Frannie pulled it up and the rest peered over her shoulders.

"We still need to find the one by the spring," Nancy said.

"What about that one?" Larry pointed to the screen.

Frannie clicked on it. "Explorer. The name doesn't tell us much." She scrolled down to the map. "It's along the lake."

"It looks like it's along the trail that goes down to the lake from the campground," Nancy said.

"There's one more in the park, clear up on the north end," Jane Ann said.

"Don't forget the one in the cemetery by the church that's across from the park." Mickey gave an eerie laugh.

"Are they all big enough to hold a turtle?" Larry asked.

"Ummm, yes. None of them are nanos," Frannie said.

Nancy took charge. "Okay, let's do two teams. Either Larry or I can be on the team that looks for the 'Spring Ahead' one because we know where we already looked the other day. But we need new eyes on it too. Ben, how about if you and Jane Ann go with Larry on that one and Frannie, Mickey and I can look for the one down by the lake."

Larry said. "Sounds like a plan, Nance. Let's go for it."

Larry, Ben and Jane Ann took off in the Shoemaker truck while Frannie loaded the coordinates for 'Explorer' in her GPS. She put her computer inside, locked the trailer and she, Mickey, and Nancy set off for the path down to the lake.

"You aren't participating in a hammer throw or log rolling contest this afternoon, Nancy?" Frannie said as they walked along the road toward the edge of the campground.

Nancy laughed. "Actually, they *are* having some kind of log event on the lake this afternoon but I've done my thing. With this wind and time of year, I bet that water is really cold and I have no wish to get dunked."

Frannie looked at the sky. "Is it supposed to rain?" she said to Mickey, their group weather guru.

"There's a chance — a front coming through and then it's supposed to start warming up."

"I can handle that," Frannie said.

Not too many people were out in the campground. Some were taking part in the contests while the rest preferred tucking in indoors. Three young boys in the next row over were having a water balloon fight. Their parents were probably just glad to have them out of the camper.

A sign with a little hiker silhouette marked the beginning of the path. Frannie led with the GPS but stepped carefully over tree roots and other obstacles on the steep descent. They reached the lakeside path and the GPS directed them to the right.

"Were there any hints with this one?" Mickey asked from the back.

"No," Nancy said.

"It says about 100 feet farther," Frannie said.

They reached a point on the path where the distance started to increase again, so began to look on the lake side of the path. Laughter and shouts came from the lake. As they neared the shore, they could see contestants trying to balance on floating logs along the other side of the lake near the beach. Wind milling arms and shouts preceded splashes into the water. The picturesque stone beach house with its round tower stood guard in the background.

Mickey craned his neck to see the screen of the GPS.

"It says it is 14 feet that way," Frannie said.

"That would put it in the lake," Mickey said. "Right. It's either underwater or the GPS is wrong."

"It's usually off a little." Frannie sidestepped down the slope toward the lake, watching the screen.

"Frannie!" Nancy cautioned but it was too late. Frannie stepped on a log that rested only partially on the land. She did a little wind milling herself but Mickey grabbed her arm and she pulled back with only her right leg soaked to the knee.

"Oh, damn, that's cold," she said.

"Do you want to go back?" Nancy asked.

"No, let's look around a little first." She squeezed water out of the bottom of her jeans.

"Are you sure you typed the coordinates in correctly?" Nancy said.

"Well, too late now. I'm not going back to the trailer to check."

"You should bring a tablet," Mickey said.

"No, you should bring a tablet."

Nancy pulled a slip of paper out of her pocket. "I wrote them down," she said sheepishly.

Frannie grinned. "Glad you did. Read them to me while I check."

Nancy did and Frannie said, "You're right. I had the last number as a three instead of a four."

The new reading led them back up the slope to the other side of the path. The chill in the air was growing and turning dampish. Frannie began poking around a fallen tree, trying to ignore her cold right foot. Nancy circled the area, checking the ground and the trees and shrubs. Mickey explored the route they had taken up from the path.

The fallen tree had several hollows along the side and Frannie checked each one, hoping not to find a nest of mice or other wildlife. When she got to the end, she peered into the broken, rotted wood.

"Found it," she called, and pulled a round metal canister out. "The cachers around here seem to like hollow logs." Nancy and Mickey hurried to her side.

"That's because there's so many of them. It looks big enough for a turtle," Mickey said. "Open it, open it."

"Relax," Frannie said as she unscrewed the top. There was only a roll of paper and a pencil.

"Bummer," Mickey said.

Frannie signed and dated the log and put everything back. She stood up and brushed off her knees.

"Okay, let's head back. I need dry clothes."

Mickey said, "Really, Frannie. You should stay away from water altogether. Remember that fall you took out of the canoe…"

"No, Mick, I forgot *all* about those days of pain."

"Just sayin'."

"I'll slug you later. First I'm going to change clothes."

CHAPTER FOURTEEN
LATE SATURDAY AFTERNOON

THEY TRUDGED BACK up the trail to their campsite. After Frannie found dry jeans and shoes, she logged their find on the website.

While they waited for the rest of the group, the pickup pulled up across the road at the fifth-wheel. Bob got out and came around to open the door for his wife.

"How considerate," Nancy said. "You guys could take a lesson from him."

Mickey started to protest but then they got a glimpse of Bob's wife. Her hair hung Medusa-like in wet strands along her face and her orange shirt and black capris clung to her body. Her descent from the truck was painful to watch, as were Bob's frustrated attempts to help. They picked up snippets of her shrill scold on the wind—"I will *never*—" and "*your* stupid idea—" floated over the road.

"What do you suppose happened?" Frannie said quietly.

"Maybe she was looking for a cache, too. You got off easy," Mickey said.

"No," Nancy said. "I saw that orange shirt on one of the logrollers."

117

"Ahhhh," Frannie and Mickey said together.

Ranger Stevenson drove by slowly and gave a little wave.

"Did we tell you that he was engaged to Frank Leslie's daughter at one point?" Frannie said.

"So is he a suspect too?" Mickey asked.

"I don't know. He says Frank Leslie forced his daughter to break it off. Could be a motive."

Ben's pickup arrived and the other team got out with cheers and bows.

Frannie sat forward. "Did you find the other turtle?"

"No, but we found our cache," Larry said.

"Well, big deal. So did we," Mickey said. "And Frannie—"

"Hush," Frannie said. "There aren't too many possibilities left."

"The women are making chili tonight, right?" Ben said.

"Yes, we are," Jane Ann said. "It'll be ready in an hour."

"Or two," said Frannie.

"Or three," Nancy said.

"Three's good," said Jane Ann.

"Very funny," Mickey said. "Har, har. What are you thinking, Ben?"

"The guys could go look for the one in the north end of the park while the girls are cooking."

"Excellent plan." Frannie opened her laptop and they copied the coordinates into one of the Garmins.

Mickey said, "Let's roll." Ben and Larry groaned. Larry added some wood to the smoldering fire first and they climbed in Ben's truck and left.

Frannie returned to a discussion of the suspects. "I think Frank's daughter, Tracy, might have been at the farm when we stopped there yesterday to give the sheriff the Geocache log. Ranger Stevenson said Frank forced the end of the engagement to Tracy by threatening to cut her off. She agreed because she hoped to reconcile with her dad but that didn't happen either."

"Sooo," Jane Ann said. "Zach seems to be a suspect and maybe the ranger."

"And maybe the daughter," Nancy said.

"True. And Darius. Larry just told me that he did actually meet Frank Leslie before Leslie died," Frannie said.

"Really? Losing your life savings or retirement or whatever surely could be a motive," said Nancy.

"What about the other daughter?" Jane Ann said. "Weren't there two?"

"Yeah," Frannie said. "That's another aspect. She's in an institution and some in town think it's because Brian — the murdered kid — attacked her. And the sheriff's wife mentioned again the people who are upset about the ethanol plant."

"Wow. No shortage of suspects," Jane Ann said. "We'd better get the chili started in case the guys find that cache in record time. We'll never hear the end of it if they get back and we haven't started. Could even be another murder. I have ground beef. Frannie, you brought tomato sauce?"

"Homemade." She was pretty proud of it considering it was the only preserving she did from her small garden.

"I'll get my kettle and I brought sausage and beans," Nancy said.

Frannie added more wood to the fire and brought out several containers of tomato sauce. They got the chili going and pulled their chairs closer to the fire.

"My money's on Zach Leslie," Jane Ann said. "Especially if there's some connection between him and the young man who died, and I would assume he had the most to gain by his father's death. He certainly isn't broken up about it."

"Does he live around here?" Nancy said.

"No, he lives in Chicago," Frannie said. "And says he wasn't here Thursday night. He came Friday morning after he got the call about his dad. But Chicago is only a few hours. He could have been here Thursday and gone back home. Kristine said that Normadean saw lights on in the house Thursday night after Frank died."

"Whoa" Nancy said. "That does sound fishy."

"It does," Frannie said, "but almost too convenient. I'm really worried about Darius, though. He didn't indicate at any time that he had talked to Frank Leslie. That concern about sleeping in the popup with a murderer on the loose could easily have been just for show. But if he's the culprit, I can't imagine that Odee knew anything about it. She seems so sweet."

"Appearances can be deceiving," Jane Ann said.

Frannie sighed. "I know."

They were all silent for a few minutes, thinking about their new acquaintance. Frannie went to get a glass of wine. When she returned, Nancy had fixed a hot cider and warmed up a bean dip that she made earlier. Jane Ann added chips. Talk shifted to the city council mess at home and then back to the murder.

"Seems like the cross-country run through the woods might not be such a good idea," Jane Ann said.

"Oh I don't know," Frannie said. "All of the suspects had personal motives. It wasn't a random killing."

"We don't know that. That's another possibility," Jane Ann insisted.

Frannie considered and Nancy got up to stir the chili. "I guess you're right. In that case, it would be foolish to have the race. But Normadean's pretty determined."

"I think the chili's ready anytime they show up," Nancy said. Big drops began to fall as if to punctuate her statement. Frannie jumped up and examined the sky.

"We'd better get stuff put away." She grabbed her lawn chair and shoved it under their camper. "We can eat in our camper." Using gloves, she hauled the pot into the trailer. Nancy and Jane Ann put their chairs under Ferraros' camper and followed Frannie in with their drinks and snacks.

Inside, Frannie cleared her laptop off the table and got out bowls and spoons.

"Do you have crackers?" Jane Ann asked.

121

"I do."

Nancy's phone rang. Her conversation was brief and when she got off the phone said, "They're on their way."

Thunder crashed and rain pelted the trailer roof, making conversation almost impossible. Frannie got out a couple of old TV trays to supplement the dinette seating. The men stomped in and Frannie threw them a couple of ratty towels. Soon everyone was holding a bowl of fragrant chili and nestled on the couch or at the dinette.

"So," Jane Ann said, fanning her mouth a little, "what's the report? Did you find the cache?"

"We did," Larry said, "but no turtle."

"Rats," said Frannie. "So we've eliminated all of the ones in the park, haven't we?"

"Right. There's one in the cemetery nearby and one in town," Ben said.

"I guess there's also the possibility that one of the nanos in the park that we didn't look for is mislabeled," Nancy said.

"True," Mickey said, and then looked up at the ceiling. "I think the rain has stopped."

As quickly as it had started, the machine-gun rattle on the roof ceased. When they finished eating, Frannie assigned cleanup to the men and got her laptop back out. Larry had propped the outside door open again, and she could hear the hiss of occasional sprinkles against the new leaves. While Jane Ann and Nancy returned their items and food to their own campers, she pulled up the list of caches again. The one in the cemetery still seemed the next best bet.

Back outside, she was surprised at the warm, humid air after the cold windy day. An eerie golden light enveloped the campground. It reminded her of those peek boxes she had made in grade school with colored tissue over the top of a shoe box to diffuse the light and a little, primitive diorama inside. The men finished their chores and trooped out behind her.

"Wow!" said Mickey. "They said a warm front. I guess they were right. We could go check out the cemetery now before dark."

"It's pretty wet," Larry said.

"They mow cemeteries. It won't be that bad. Who's game?"

"Well, Normadean wanted help again tomorrow. I didn't commit, but I suppose it wouldn't hurt to try and find that one tonight. We've got about an hour and half of daylight."

Ben and Nancy opted to sit this one out—Frannie thought that in spite of their conditioning, they were starting to look a little weary after the morning's race. So the other four piled in the Shoemaker truck with jackets, small LED flashlights, and Garmins in hand.

CHAPTER FIFTEEN
EARLY SATURDAY EVENING

THE CEMETERY WAS on the same side of the park as the Leslie farm, father south along the gravel road. It sat behind an old wooden church on a corner. The church faced the side road with its own drive; Larry pulled in to the cemetery entrance further along the park road. By the time they got there, fog was settling in and the visibility had dropped.

"Spooooky," Mickey said.

"Maybe we *should* come back tomorrow," Jane Ann said.

"Chicken," her husband replied and opened the truck door. They got out and Frannie tried to concentrate on the Garmin screen rather than the looming, gnarled junipers and tilting gravestones. The little country church huddled to one side, with windows boarded up and sadly needing paint. Fog always felt like the rest of the world had disappeared and all that remained was contained in a hundred-foot circle.

"Let's get this over with," Frannie said and switched on her flashlight. She tripped on a small headstone that was almost flush with the ground. Larry caught her and she pointed in the direction indicated by the Garmin.

"That way, I guess. About 80 feet." She kept her flashlight pointed at the ground to avoid any more mishaps. It wasn't dark yet but the fog seemed to be thickening by the minute. Moisture dripped from the trees providing an ominous soundtrack. At one point, she thought she heard low voices but decided her imagination was on overtime.

"Looks like a good place for zombies," Mickey said from behind her.

"Oh, hush," Frannie said. "I'm trying to concentrate."

"We don't want to ruin that," Mickey said, and made no further comment.

They proceeded single file. A groan came from behind her so she said again, "I said hush, Mickey."

"That wasn't me," he objected.

She swallowed but kept going. She hoped it was her imagination; otherwise she didn't want to know the source. They reached a clump of three twisted junipers. Under one a pitted headstone listed to the left, seemingly supported by a thorny rose bush just beginning to show its leaves.

"Here?" Jane Ann asked.

"Must be. It says a foot and a half." They used their flashlights to examine the trees and neighboring graves. Frannie poked around in the old rose bush with no luck.

"I feel like we're trespassing, just because the fog makes me feel so sneaky," Jane Ann said. Frannie agreed. And fog always muffled sound as well as visibility and gave the feeling of an old black-and-white movie. As she looked out from the clump of trees, the gray shroud became solid only a few feet away. Even the nearest stones were barely discernible. All color was washed out of the surrounding area.

"I think I found something," Mickey said. He pulled a small plastic container from a space under one of the tree roots. They gathered around as he opened it. Inside was a scrap of paper, a pencil, and a star-shaped token.

"Oh, man," said Mickey. "It's a zombie hunter geocoin. I don't have anything to put in its place. Wish I did; that is cool."

"Then you'll have to leave it. No turtles, though. Sign the log so we can get back to camp," Larry said.

Mickey was writing his name with his flashlight between his teeth when they heard a shout of "No!" They straightened and listened, looking at each other with wide eyes.

"What was that?" Jane Ann whispered. They strained to stare into the fog as if that would improve their vision. But the distortion of sound had them looking in different directions.

They heard a pop, followed by another groan and running footsteps.

"Over by the church? That was a gunshot," Larry said, keeping his voice low.

"I thought it came from the other direction," Jane Ann said.

"Well, let's head toward the truck. Stay low, but they can't see us if we can't see them."

"What if someone's hurt, Larry?" Frannie said.

"We'll call the sheriff from the truck. That was definitely a gunshot. We don't even know where. And it wouldn't be smart to go wandering around in this fog when someone has a gun out there."

It was almost full dark now, making the return to the truck even more treacherous. A moan came out of the fog again from somewhere and in the distance a car started and drove away. Frannie hung on to the back of Larry's jacket as he led the way between the tombstones. In places, the fog parted, like it was going to lift, and then closed in on them again. They reached the truck, got in, and Larry locked the doors. He started the truck, and turned on the headlights.

The beams were strong enough to barely pick out the hulk of the little church off to their right. Larry pulled out his phone and dialed 911.

Mickey peered into the fog. "There's someone on the ground there by the corner of the church."

Frannie and Jane Ann looked where he pointed and could only make out a shapeless heap on the ground.

"It could just be a pile of old clothes or something," Jane Ann said.

"I don't think so. I saw it move."

Larry finished his call, turned off the truck and handed the keys to Mickey. "The sheriff is nearby. Get me my gun out of the glove box."

Mickey did, along with a small box of ammunition and handed it to Larry. They had seen no further movement from the pile of clothes. He switched off the lights.

"I'm going over there. Leave the lights off."

"Larry —," Frannie began.

"I'll be fine. We heard a car leave; I think the danger's over."

"Then we can go with you," she said.

"No," he said firmly. "You'll be able to see my flashlight. Direct the sheriff when he gets here. Shouldn't be long." He slid out of the truck and was gone.

Frannie rolled down her window and followed the little pinpoint of light. Then the fog swallowed the light — at least she hoped that was the cause of its disappearance. Her stomach dropped and a lump formed in her throat.

"Oh, Mickey," she said, "what if —?" but then the light reappeared, headed back to the truck. She took a deep breath and at the same time a siren cut through the fog.

"That was quick," Mickey said.

Larry materialized and opened the truck door. He turned the headlights back on.

"Frannie, get the first aid kit from under the back seat."

She handed it to him. "Who is it? Do you know?"

"Zach Leslie." He opened the kit on the driver seat.

"Was he shot?" Jane Ann said.

"What was he doing here?" Mickey asked at the same time.

Larry held up a hand. "One at a time. He was shot in the leg. I have no idea what he was doing here. Maybe geocaching." He looked up from the kit and gave a wry smile. The sheriff's car pulled up alongside the truck, the flashing red and blue lights casting an even eerier glow than usual.

He met the sheriff in the front of the truck, talking quickly and pointing to where Zach Leslie lay. They took off at a jog toward the church, Larry with a bottle of antiseptic in one hand and Sheriff Jackson speaking into his shoulder mike.

Frannie said, "I'm getting out. There can't be much danger with all of this going on." Mickey and Jane Ann followed and they walked toward the church, stopping a little ways back from the huddle around Leslie. The headlights from the truck and the sheriff's car improved visibility in the immediate area. The sheriff was bent over, speaking to Leslie when the ambulance pulled up, but Frannie couldn't make out what was being said.

Larry and Jackson stood back to let the EMTs do their thing. Zach Leslie appeared to be going in and out of consciousness. As the ambulance pulled out, the sheriff and Larry walked back to the rest of the group.

"So this was another of those geocache things?" The sheriff looked skeptical.

"Yessir, and we found it," Mickey said.

"Did any of you see or hear anything else?"

Frannie waved at the fog surrounding them. "By the time we got here, we could barely see in front of our faces. We did hear some noises but I thought we were just getting spooked by the cemetery."

"What kind of noises did you hear?" The sheriff narrowed his eyes at Frannie.

"Um, well, first I thought I heard voices when we were looking for the cache. So low that I couldn't make out any words and I decided it was just branches rubbing together or the old church settling or something." She looked at the others for confirmation, but they all shrugged.

"Then it sounded like a moan and I accused Mickey of trying to spook me but he said it wasn't him."

The sheriff looked at Mickey and the others; this time they nodded in confirmation.

"Then right after we found the cache, we all heard someone yell 'No!,' the shot and another groan."

"We did," Jane Ann confirmed. "And footsteps. After the shot, we heard someone hurrying away."

"And then a car started," added Mickey.

"Did Zach know who shot him?" Frannie said.

Larry shook his head. "He said the guy had a ski mask on."

"So it was a man?" Frannie said.

Larry shrugged. "He thinks so."

"Well, I've got to get to the hospital," the sheriff said. "I *strongly* suggest you folks return to the campground. I'll stop by later and see if you remember anything else."

"On our way," Larry said, and the others were not reluctant to follow. A breeze had picked up and lifted the fog somewhat. As they pulled onto the gravel road, Frannie noticed Zach Leslie's big white Hummer parked on the other side of the church.

CHAPTER SIXTEEN

SATURDAY NIGHT

ON THE RIDE back, Frannie leaned forward from the rear seat and pelted Larry with questions.

"Did Zach say what he was doing out here?"

"I didn't ask. He could barely talk."

"But he must have been talking to the person right before he was shot. You'd think he'd have some idea who it was."

"He says not. I don't know any more than that."

She sat back in her seat and mulled over the events.

"The fog seems to be lifting," Mickey said. "'Course it could be just lighter here. Fog is funny that way — thick here — thin there."

"Yeah, yeah," Larry said, and Mickey shut up.

Frannie noticed the Lumleys' SUV parked beside their popup as they passed. Nancy and Ben had gotten the fire going again after the rain and sat in lounge chairs, mesmerized by the flames.

"Hey," Ben said as they got out of the truck. "Did we hear sirens again? You guys didn't mug an old lady, did you?"

"We *are* old ladies," Jane Ann said.

Mickey launched into a colorful description of their search and the subsequent shooting, only slightly exaggerated.

Both Ben and Nancy sat up in their chairs. "Wow," Ben said. "Fog, huh? It hasn't been that bad here."

"What did I tell ya?" Mickey said.

"I believe I'm ready for a beer," Larry said, pulling one of the chairs from under the trailer. He got seated and Cuba nuzzled up for a scratch. Frannie went in for a glass of wine and a fleece blanket. It had warmed up but the air was damp and she still felt the effects of the chilly day. When she got back outside, the Lumleys were coming up the road walking Peaches. Nancy invited them to join the group again and more chairs were produced.

Odee took a seat next to Frannie. "How was your day?"

"We helped with the 5K run this morning and did a little geocaching this afternoon." Frannie grinned. "And some much needed napping."

"Have you heard any more about the murder? Have they caught anybody?" Odee said. She twisted her hands together as she asked.

"Not really. There's quite a few suspects." She paused. "There was a shooting a little while ago just outside the park." She watched Odee's face as she said it.

"Oh! Darius said he saw the ambulance and sheriff's car. He went to town for ice and saw them as he drove back. A shooting? This is getting scary."

So Darius had opportunity, Frannie thought.

"What do you think is going on?" Odee said.

"I don't know. There seems to be a lot of old grudges as well as new problems with this ethanol plant. It's a muddle. Have you found out any more about your land?"

Odee twisted her hands more. "Well, just that it's definitely *not* our land. Live and learn I guess."

"I'm really sorry."

"Thank you. I think we will start back home tomorrow. The silver lining is that we found this park and met you folks. We'd better continue on our walk. It was really great to meet you." She got up and Frannie did also. Odee leaned over and gave her a hug.

Darius shook hands with the men and everyone joined in wishing them a safe journey.

After they were gone, Frannie said to Larry, "So if they can leave, Darius must have been cleared of any suspicion."

Larry shrugged. "I'm not sure the sheriff knows that he met with Frank Leslie."

"Larry! You've been withholding information from the authorities." Frannie couldn't resist—it was an accusation he frequently made against her.

"I know. Frankly it slipped my mind. I'd better tell him when he stops back here tonight."

"Oh, dear," Frannie said. She should have kept her mouth shut. She was sure that Darius Lumley was the least likely suspect and this would just add to his woes.

The sheriff pulled up to the campsite. He sauntered up to the group, took off his hat and rubbed his head.

"How's Zach Leslie?" Larry asked.

"He's going to be okay, but he won't be running any races."

"I don't think he's much of a runner," Frannie said.

"Anyone remember anything else about your little adventure this evening?"

There were no affirmative answers and several shakes of the heads.

"You know," Larry said, "it was quite foggy when we arrived, but we had our headlights on so I would think that if someone was already there, they would have seen us come in and gone somewhere else. On the other hand, we didn't hear any other vehicles arrive after we did."

The sheriff nodded. "According to Zach, he was already there. He saw your lights and moved behind the church. The other person arrived a few minutes later."

"Why was he there?"

"He says he got a text from a blocked number to do so."

"What about?" Frannie said. "Why would he go to meet an anonymous person some place like that? Sounds to me like he's got something to hide."

Sheriff Jackson raised his eyebrows and glanced at Larry.

"I know, I know. I need to stay out of it. But he's mixed up in this somehow." Frannie said. "If I got a text telling me to meet an anonymous person in a cemetery, I certainly wouldn't go unless I was worried about blackmail or something."

"Sounds like you're speaking from experience." The sheriff winked at Larry.

Really, this Old Boys' Club was getting too exasperating. "Well, would you?" Frannie challenged.

"Probably not. You're right." Sheriff Jackson looked at the rest of the group. "You said you heard a car leave after the shot. Could you tell what direction it was from the church?"

"South," said Mickey.

"North," said Frannie.

"Glad we got that settled," the sheriff said. "I know the fog really distorts sound. Well, let me know if you remember anything else. I need to talk to Normadean about tomorrow's schedule." He winced. "Have a good night."

He had reached his car and was getting in when Larry called after him.

"Sheriff!" He hurried to the car and Jackson rolled the window down.

Larry rested one hand on the roof of the car and leaned over, talking in a low voice. Frannie realized he was probably telling Jackson about Darius Lumley. It gave her a guilty, sinking sensation.

The sheriff drove away and Larry returned to the group. Frannie tried unsuccessfully to catch his eye. They settled back in their lawn chairs like a flock of pigeons. They discussed the shooting a little more with no new information or conclusions. They rehashed the murder with the same results. The boys from the next row were racing each other around the campground on bikes with the wheels outlined with glow sticks but other than that, the campground was peaceful.

Finally, Jane Ann said, "It has been one long day and my bed is calling." She was just folding up her camp chair, when the hum of a golf cart made them all turn toward the road.

Normadean, back in her blue sweat suit, dismounted and grabbed her ever-present clipboard "Glad I caught you before you turned in!"

Jane Ann groaned.

"I just got done talking to the sheriff and we're going ahead with the cross-country run tomorrow so I need more volunteers."

"Did the route have to be changed?" Frannie said.

"Just in one area. No biggie. Will any of you help me out? It's a good cause."

"On one condition," Larry said. "Put us all in the same area." Then he turned to the rest. "That okay? None of you are in the race, are you?"

Even Ben shook his head. "Sounds like a sprained ankle to me."

Normadean waved off that silly idea. "Great. We're postponing until 10:00 in case this fog hangs on. Be at the registration area by 9:30 — "

Several loud pops sounded behind her. Her eyes went wide and her face pale as she dropped to the ground.

"What the—" From her hands and knees, she looked wildly around. Larry had jumped up, but the others had also ducked, trying to determine the source.

Smothered laughter from behind a nearby tree gave them their answer.

"Hey! You boys! Do I need to talk to your parents?" Larry shouted.

"No!" came back, more giggles and circles of glow sticks vanished into the night.

Mickey and Ben went to help Normadean up.

"Are you okay?" Ben asked.

She roughly brushed off her sweat suit. "Damn kids! I'll catch them later. There's no excuse for that kind of behavior. They aren't supposed to have firecrackers here anyway."

In spite of her bravado, Frannie noticed she dripped with sweat and shook as she tried to hold her pencil to her clipboard. She took their names and no other information—either she was too upset or more likely, had everything else on file or on her hard drive.

"See you tomorrow." She abruptly turned and hightailed it for the golf cart.

"Kind of an extreme reaction," Mickey said.

"I agree." Frannie folded up her own chair and said her good nights to the group.

BY THE TIME Larry came in she had brushed her teeth and gotten into some flannel pajamas, still trying to warm her chilly bones.

Larry got a pot of coffee ready for the morning. "This *is* a pretty odd case," he finally said.

She jerked her head up, surprised that he would bring it up.

"It is," she said, trying to sound only half interested. "What do you think about Normadean?"

"Think about her? I'm glad I'm not her husband. You mean in connection to this case?"

"Sort of. I don't think she murdered Frank Leslie. I don't know why she would. But I'm wondering if she shot Zach."

"Why?"

"Welll…" Frannie plopped down on the couch. "She told that Ed guy in the bar last night that she thought his brother's murder would be resolved soon. Or settled—I don't remember exactly her words. And the first time I saw her, she was facing away from me and I thought she was a man. If Zach's attacker was wearing a ski mask, he might think that too."

"Go on."

"Her reaction tonight to that noise. Yesterday, she didn't think all of the sheriff's worry about the race was justified. Now all of a sudden, she seemed to think someone was shooting at her. Why?"

Larry looked at her with almost admiration. "You may have something there."

"Really?"

"And I intend to think about it more tomorrow. Right now, I'm going to bed."

CHAPTER SEVENTEEN
SUNDAY MORNING

EARLY MORNING WITH the sun just coming up and only a few fellow campers stirring was usually the perfect peaceful way to start a day. Frannie savored her first cup of coffee and sometimes read but often just watched the campground wake up.

There was no sun this morning. Or if there was, it was obliterated by the fog, which had thickened again overnight. She could hear doors opening and occasional low voices but couldn't see much beyond their own camping circle.

With few distractions, her thoughts returned to the events of the night before. It was obvious that there was no shortage of people who didn't care for Zach Leslie. If Zach told the sheriff the truth — and she had her doubts about anything he said — someone lured him to the old church for no other reason than to harm him. Was Normadean really capable of that? She had seemed like the typical OCD community organizer, but there was something much more complex beneath the surface.

Frannie opened her book and read a couple of chapters. The sun struggled to break through the fog without much success. Some familiar giggles interrupted the chase scene in her mystery. She looked up just as two of the boys from the night before came around the end of the trailer. They stopped short with a deer in the headlights look on their faces when they realized she was sitting there. They started to edge backwards.

"Say," Frannie said. "Come here a minute. I just want to talk to you."

One, a redhead, wore camouflage pajamas and the other, a towhead, sported baggy shorts with an oversized football jersey. They both looked like their hair had been stirred with a spoon. They came a little closer but well out of Frannie's reach, in case she took a notion to grab them. She must look tougher than she thought.

"You know, you really frightened that lady last night. I know you were just having fun but you don't want to give someone a heart attack, do you?"

Their smirks dissolved and they looked at each other and shook their heads.

"Is that—that why the cops are here?" asked the redhead. He looked to be the older, about nine.

"The cops are here?" Frannie said.

"Down that way," said the towhead, and pointed in the direction of the Lumleys' camper.

"I doubt it," Frannie said. "Just don't do it again or they *will* be looking for you."

They both said, "Okay!" and turned and ran. Frannie got up and walked to the other end of the trailer where she could see more of the road. Or at least where the road should be. The fog obscured the popup but she could see the flashing lights from a patrol car. The authorities were definitely at the Lumleys' campsite.

Heavily, she headed back toward her chair. Larry came out of the camper with his coffee mug.

"What's happenin'?" he said as he stretched.

"The sheriff is down at the Lumleys," Frannie said.

"Oh." He looked just a tad bit guilty. "I had no choice, Frannie. I had to report it."

She sighed. "I know, but..." She couldn't explain the 'but.'

"Yeah." he said. He walked out toward the road and stared into the fog.

She refilled her own mug and went back to her book but couldn't concentrate. Mickey bounced out of his motorhome.

"I've got smashed potatoes in the oven and sausage gravy warming up. We need sustenance if we're going to survive more grueling duty this morning." He noticed their faces. "What's up?"

Frannie told him and he turned serious.

"Do you think they'll arrest him, Larry?"

Larry shrugged. "I don't know what all evidence they've gathered. But from what we've seen, there's at least a couple of other good possibilities. I'm guessing they'll just tell him to stay put until they know more."

"Darius'll know the information came from us," Frannie said.

"He didn't tell me how he met Frank. Maybe there are other witnesses."

141

"You wish."

Mickey hesitated and then said, "Breakfast will be in about ten minutes. Maybe that will help."

"Okay, I'll cut up some fruit for our contribution," Frannie said.

They went about their tasks in silence. Nancy and Ben brought over some yogurt and granola.

"It cancels out some of that sausage gravy, health-wise," Nancy said.

Breakfast was excellent but conversation was subdued. They discussed what they could possibly do to help the Lumleys but couldn't come up with anything.

"We need to remember that there is a small chance that he *is* the killer," Larry said. Nobody replied.

After breakfast, while Larry helped Mickey and Jane Ann with the dishes, Frannie and Nancy took the dogs for a walk. The fog created little dioramas at each campsite, to be revealed only as they neared. Some sites were quiet, some busy with the rituals of breakfast, and some in a flurry of packing up to head home. When they got to Lumleys' site, Odee was unpacking a few things they had already stowed in their truck before they found out they weren't leaving. She turned around when she heard their approach. Her face froze, and she turned back to her task without speaking.

"Oh, boy," Frannie said, as they continued on. "I don't know what to say to her."

"Me either," Nancy said.

FRANNIE FRETTED ABOUT it on the ride over to the registration shelter but couldn't come up with any way of comforting or reassuring Odee. The fog was thinning and people were milling around the shelter. Her group gathered in one corner waiting for assignments. Normadean was in her take-charge mode but seemed a little less sure of herself, even somewhat distracted, than on the other days. She called for attention and handed out copies of maps of the park.

"Now," she said firmly. "This route should be challenging but a lot of fun for the runners. They'll start out down by the east entrance. They'll go out the entrance road and down the lane to Bob Greiner's farm, run through the barn, jump or climb over some hay bales that we've set up, go across the bean field, over the fence and back into the park on the Acorn hiking path. It goes along the road to the C parking area. Flags mark the route through the woods down to where it picks up the Lake Trail. From there, they'll take the Cliff Trail, come back out, and along the road to the stream—but they can't use the bridge to cross; they have to go through the water."

Several of the volunteers looked at each other and shivered.

"We'll finish up at the Balanced Rock. Everyone know where that is?" She held up her copy of the map and pointed.

Satisfied that they weren't going to be completely lost, she went on. "I need you people to do several things. First, make sure everyone stays on course and

TO CACHE A KILLER

doesn't make a wrong turn. Also be available in case we have any injuries. There's some tricky terrain."

"Tricky?" Nancy said in low voice. "That's an understatement. I'm so glad I didn't sign up for this."

Normadean frowned at her and continued. "Have a cell phone handy. My number is on the bottom of this map. Those of you who are on the Cliff Trail need to make sure the runners stay away from the edge. Several people have fallen through the years and been injured or killed." She looked at their shocked faces and added, "Not during this race though."

She worked her way through the list, assigning volunteers to various segments of the racecourse. Frannie's group was among those assigned to the Cliff Trail. They had hiked this trail several times. It ran along a spine of dolomite rock that had been carved into a high peninsula by a loop in the river. The beginning of the spine was narrow with very little rock separating either side of the trail from the cliff's edge. This was where most of the falls had happened in the past. The peninsula widened out closer to the river and the trail made a loop near the edge and came back to itself.

"Excuse me?" Frannie raised her hand.

Normadean nodded at her.

"Aren't we going to have people going both directions on the first part of the Cliff Trail?"

"Absolutely. That's one of the obstacles and that's why we need volunteers there especially. There won't be as many runners today as yesterday and by the time they reach the Cliff Trail, they should be pretty spread out. There are two places where the trail splits and you can direct the returning runners to go to the left. Any other questions?"

Frannie looked at the others and she could tell that they all thought this whole thing was a bad idea.

Normadean wasn't done. "Immediately after, we will meet back here and hand out the awards for all events."

A white Hummer pulled up in the parking area and Zach Leslie got out, pulling a pair of crutches out behind him. He swung up the grassy slope to the shelter and stood outside, staring at Normadean.

She ignored him while she continued assignments, but dropped her pencil twice and gave two groups the same area by mistake. Finally, she looked over at Zach.

"Did you want something, Mr. Leslie?"

"I thought I might run in the race." He smirked. Frannie glanced at Larry and saw that he was watching the exchange intently.

Normadean flushed and turned away from him. He laughed and hobbled back to his car.

"Something's definitely going on there," Larry said.

"Ya think?" Mickey said.

They got in their trucks to drive to the parking area nearest the Cliff Trail. On their route, they passed the C parking area, where the sheriff had taken Larry and Frannie on Friday morning. At the slow speed limit maintained in the park, they could see new flags going into the woods and angling away from the crime scene.

"I wonder who set up the route in the first place," Jane Ann said. "I'm guessing somebody who doesn't run."

"Probably Normadean," Frannie said. "I think she pretty much controls this whole thing."

Other volunteers were already in the Cliff Trail parking lot. Normadean must have a lot of connections to get so many people out on such a gloomy Sunday. The local churches had to be pretty empty this morning.

They moved along the trail, stepping carefully to avoid the small but treacherous fissures snaking in from the cliff's edge. In places, the narrow trail wound around boulders and outcroppings and required concentration to keep the precarious footing. The fog was almost gone but the trees dripped with condensation, like glass beads along the branches. The rocks, which Frannie sometimes grabbed to keep her balance, were slippery and didn't offer much purchase.

"This is nuts," she said. "What is Normadean thinking?"

CHAPTER EIGHTEEN
SUNDAY MID-MORNING

THEY REACHED A stretch where no volunteers were posted. Frannie took a spot in an open area where the ridge widened out. But she noticed with trepidation that five or six feet behind her a bigger crevasse ran parallel to the trail with dead trees growing out of the sides. She would need to remember not to back up suddenly. Across from her were large boulders riddled by erosion, one with a large hole all the way through it. While she examined the rest of the area from her position, a loud "Boo!" made her jump.

Mickey's grinning face appeared in the hole in the rock across from her.

"Someday, I'm just going to kill you, Mickey."

"Keep your voice down," he said. "Witnesses. That's not very smart for a detective."

"I'm not a detective."

"Try to remember that," came Larry's voice from behind another large boulder further down the trail. "Mickey, quit screwing around and find a place where you can be useful."

"I'm not sure that's possible," Frannie said.

"Geesh! No one appreciates me." He climbed down from behind the boulders.

Ben, on the other side of Larry, yelled "Down here, Mick!"

Frannie found an outcropping that made a tolerable seat and she sat down to wait.

"It's going to be a while," Jane Ann said. "Only 10:00 now." She leaned against a tree about fifteen feet from Frannie.

"I should have brought a book," Frannie grumbled.

"At least the sun is coming out and the scenery is great."

"I just wish some of the scenery wasn't so far down there," Frannie said, pointing over towards the edge of the cliff. But she looked around and found the immediate vista very pleasing. The sun filtered through the new leaves on the trees, the fresh green leaves contrasting with the ancient gray rocks.

They heard voices. "That can't be runners already, can it?" Frannie said.

"No, and by the time they get here, they won't be able to talk anyway," Jane Ann said.

The trail curved right before their positions and Frannie was surprised to see Normadean round the corner, walking no less. Of course, it was hardly a suitable track for a golf cart. But she carried her ever-present clipboard.

She nodded as she saw their spacing and checked something off on the clipboard.

"I'm going to be where the trail loops back to join this part and I'll direct traffic there. If you have a conflict between two runners, let the leaders through first."

"Kind of like giving the rich bigger tax breaks," Jane Ann muttered after she was gone up the trail. Frannie snickered.

They chatted while they waited and Nancy distributed homemade granola bars. Jane Ann mentioned a geocache on the trail that they had hunted on an earlier trip a few years before and never found.

"Maybe it's the other turtle," Nancy said.

"I don't think so," Frannie said. "I noticed it on the list and nobody else has found it for a couple of years. It says it 'needs maintenance.' Besides, it's a micro."

Arguments punctuated by laughter came from farther up the trail where Larry, Mickey and Ben were.

"Wouldn't you think they'd get tired of it?" Jane Ann said.

"They thrive on it. Ow!" Frannie slapped her neck. "The gnats are out and fierce."

Nancy handed around a bottle of vanilla.

Finally they heard some cheering coming from the direction of the parking lot. The noise moved closer and a young woman appeared around the corner. Her gait couldn't be classified as running. Strands of hair escaped from her ponytail flopped around her face. She kept her eyes on the ground to avoid mishap and didn't acknowledge their shouts of encouragement. Her panting was audible over the noise and as she passed, they saw that the backs of her legs and her shorts were splattered with mud.

A few others followed her in much the same shape and widely separated. Frannie recognized Mark Masters, the protester, as one of the front-runners. The numbers increased but still single file. They focused more on just finishing rather than time.

The next group was a little closer together and moving more at a fast walk. Most of the women appeared to be twenty-somethings, while there were more thirties and forties among the men. Mud splatter was everywhere and bits of hay accessorized some of the spandex.

During a lull, Ranger Stevenson appeared around the corner. In contrast to the runners, he looked sharp and pressed and carried his weight in tools around his belt.

"Ranger," Frannie called out, "Are you in the race?"

He smiled, a little flustered as if he wasn't quite sure she was kidding.

"Uh, no. Just checking things."

"So far, so good," Jane Ann said.

He nodded and hurried on past them but stopped to visit with the men a minute. A gnat found the only spot on Frannie's ear that she had missed with the vanilla. The sun was warming things up so she took off her hoodie and tied the sleeves around her waist. They applauded the next group of runners, and then there was another quiet spell. Between the warm sun and the stress of the night before, Frannie was afraid if she sat down on her rock, she would doze off. It should be about time for the first runners to be coming back.

A scream brought her fully alert. Larry headed down the path toward the sound faster than any of the runners had. Frannie followed and saw Ben ahead of Larry.

She said to Jane Ann as she passed, "You and Nancy better stay here in case more runners come along." She soon fell behind the men as she tried to navigate the rough terrain without taking a header.

Ben and Larry had stopped where the loop at the end of the peninsula joined the path. They were looking down at the side of the path, pointing and in serious discussion. Ranger Stevenson was hurrying back along one arm of the loop, not looking nearly as cool and spiffy as he had earlier. He arrived at the same time she did.

Along the path was another of the frequent crevasses and looking into it, she saw Normadean's pain-contorted face. She was crying and gripping the upper edge with her right hand. Ben dropped to his stomach and coaxed her to give him her other hand. Larry had his phone out and was calling for help.

"My foot!" she sobbed. "It's caught!"

The ranger took charge and worked his way down into the crevasse from the wider end. He ducked down to examine her foot and popped back up.

"It's really wedged in there," he said to Larry. "Tell them to bring something we can use to break that hold. I'm going to see what I can do to keep her from slipping farther." Then to Ben, "Find me a solid branch or something."

Frannie said to no one in particular, "Do you want me to stop the runners as they come around the loop and hold them there?"

Normadean said, "No, don't stop the race." But she was pleading, not giving orders.

"I'll take names in the order they reach me and you can either use that as the final results or restart it later. Where's your clipboard?"

She became more frantic. "Ohhh, I don't know!" She tried to twist around and look behind her. "Yikes!" A look of fresh pain crossed her face.

"Don't worry—I'll find it, or something I can use," Frannie said. She sidled around Larry, still on the phone and standing in the middle of the path. Ben was handing a large branch down to the ranger.

Larry closed his phone and said to Frannie, "I'll go tell the others and have Mickey block any other runners coming from that direction."

She searched around the crevasse and finally spotted the clipboard caught in a shrub on the edge of the crevasse. Taking no chances, she dropped to her stomach and managed to reach it.

"Ben, do you have a pen?"

He produced one without looking at her while he waited for further instructions from the ranger.

"Thanks! Normadean, I found your clipboard. Don't worry about the race."

Normadean looked up. "The list of runners is the second page. Thank you." She looked like she was about to cry again.

CHAPTER NINETEEN
LATE SUNDAY MORNING

THE RIGHT SIDE of the peninsula was lower so the trail dipped down on that side. Soon Frannie could no longer see the group trying to help Normadean. She stopped. This distance would keep the runners out of the way.

The first sheet on the clipboard listed the volunteers in alphabetical order with neat checks in columns. The second and third pages registered the names of the participants, also alphabetical, sixty-seven in all, although five were apparently no-shows because their names were not checked off. There were columns with space for times and order of finish.

While she waited, she heard more voices from the trail juncture and sounds of hammering.

Soon, pounding footsteps and heavy breathing came closer along the peninsula from her right. She glimpsed the first runner rounding the curve. There were four in the first group. Frannie stepped into the path and held up her hand.

"We have to stop the race temporarily."

Their stop was not graceful, rather like a group of rag dolls tossed in a heap except they did manage to stay upright. They bent over, hands on knees, or leaned on trees.

The young woman who had been in the lead when Frannie saw her earlier said, "Why?"

"There's been an accident. Normadean slipped into a crack and wedged her foot. We're waiting for emergency personnel to free her and get her medical attention. I need your names and I'll check off the order you came in."

They clustered around and other arrivals added to the confusion. This wasn't going to work. She reverted to teacher mode and started lining them up. Good thing it wasn't being televised. There wasn't much official about her method. The runners cooperated somewhat and got themselves in order of their positions to this point. There was only one argument about who was ahead of whom. Then the questions started.

"What happened to her?"

"Was she hurt?"

"Will we finish today or is this the final order?"

Frannie held up her hand for quiet. Too bad she didn't have a whistle. "We don't know what happened — no one saw it. Her foot is wedged between two rocks. And I have no idea what they'll do about the race. But we really appreciate your cooperation."

Mark Masters raised his hand. The teacher thing must show.

"Are you sure she wasn't pushed?

"Why would you say that? As I said, they have no idea yet how it happened."

"She's been pretty vocal against the ethanol plant and there's plenty of thugs around who are favor of it."

A stocky, dark-haired man in his thirties leaned forward and looked down the line at Masters. "What do you mean, thugs? Wanting to help the economy around here doesn't make anyone a thug."

Frannie looked at him closer. He looked familiar. She was pretty sure he was one of the men who had been at the bar with Zach Leslie.

"It's the way you're going about it that makes you thugs. Besides, it's raping the environment," Masters said.

"You creepy little tree-hugger." The man almost spat the words. He started toward Masters but a man next to him grabbed his arm.

"Not here," the man said quietly.

Chatter picked up in the rest of the group even though it appeared that many of them didn't know each other. Frannie kept her eye on Masters and the dark-haired man, but they had cooled down. Obviously emotions were running high about the ethanol plant. Maybe Frank Leslie's murder *was* tied up with that rather than Darius Lumley's purchase, Ranger Stevenson's engagement, or Brian Murray's death. Mark Masters was an impetuous hothead.

She looked at the list of runners and at the line of people. If she had the order right, the dark-haired man's name was Cody Stanley. She flipped through the other pages. There were precise charts of events, participants, and results. Normadean had used different colors of ink to record some information and only she knew the meaning. But on the margin several pages back a note jumped off the page—a violation of all that order. It read *ZL 7:00.*

That was about the time they had been in the cemetery the night before. 'ZL' had to be Zach Leslie—there couldn't be too many people in the area with those initials. Could Normadean actually have been Zach's assailant? And could there be any reason why Zach would keep it quiet if he knew that?

Her reverie was interrupted by Larry's appearance. He waited until he reached her to give his report.

"They got her out and the EMTs took her to the nearest clinic. She might have a broken ankle. But you can let the runners go on and she can decide later what she wants to do about results. You got their current order down?" He nodded toward the clipboard.

"Yeah." She showed him the sheet. She turned to the runners and raised her voice. "Okay, the way is cleared and the race is going to continue. On the count of three." She counted out slowly, thinking this was probably not a proper restart but too bad.

As they took off, several jockeying for position on the narrow path, she and Larry backed off the path to let them pass. There was some muttering among the front-runners about the spacing, but Frannie smiled at them and said, "Hey, it's for a good cause!" She hoped that was true.

After the last one had passed, she showed Larry the sheet with Normadean's note on it.

"Do you suppose this means last night?"

"Could be, I suppose."

"Well, supposedly Zach wasn't in town until Friday and Friday night we were all at the bar. Normadean certainly wasn't meeting with him then."

"Right."

She also told him about Mark Masters' suggestion that Normadean may have been pushed.

"I imagine the sheriff will question her about that," Larry said.

"Not if she tells him it was just an accident. She's hiding something."

She followed him back to the trail junction. Ben had taken over Normadean's post there. Other runners were coming down the path toward the loop. Frannie returned to her post and filled Jane Ann and Nancy in on the recent events as they sat on the rocks.

"Maybe we should go visit Normadean when we get done here," Nancy said with a grin. "You know, report in and stuff. I have some cookies we could take her."

"Now that's a sacrifice. Those are good cookies," Jane Ann said.

Runners were coming from both directions and Nancy jumped up.

"I'd better get back on the job and direct one of these groups down the other path."

For the next half hour, they were busy. Finally a man Frannie had never seen came along.

"That's the last. As soon as they make the loop and come back out, you're done. We really appreciate your help. We're going to move the awards to this evening because of Normadean's accident. Please tell the runners it will be at 7:00 and there will be free ice cream."

Frannie nodded and gave him Normadean's clipboard and he moved on.

"So how do we know when they've all come out?" Jane Ann said.

"We watch for that woman in the Minnie Mouse shirt. She was in the last group," Nancy said.

"Unless she has a big spurt right before the finish," Frannie said. The other two stuck out their tongues at her.

By the time they were back in the trucks, Frannie was ready for a soft seat and some lunch.

"What say we grab something in town?" Mickey suggested. He had no trouble convincing the rest.

CHAPTER TWENTY
SUNDAY EARLY AFTERNOON

THEY DROVE DOWN the main street of Blueberry Hill, checking out the possibilities. Nancy spotted an unimposing box of a building sporting a hand-lettered sign in the window that read 'Chinese Food, Ice Cream, and Crafts.' The restaurant did not appear to have an official name, but the parking lot was full, which they considered a good sign. Ben turned his truck into a parking place and Larry followed.

"Wow!" Mickey said. "How can we go wrong? You girls can get in some early Christmas shopping after we feast on Peking duck and a little tin roof sundae."

Inside the room was crowded with laminated tables and mismatched chrome chairs. Shelves lined the walls loaded with an array of items fit for a Turkish bazaar. It looked like the handmade items had been collected over several decades. Frannie recognize 'glass grapes' like she and her mother had made from resin in the Sixties. Dolls sported huge crocheted skirts and cat-shaped clocks with moving eyes and tails ticked away with plodding determination. Macramé owls perched alongside hand printed and knitted scarves. Silk flower arrangements were interspersed with racks holding stone necklaces and earrings.

The clientele presented the same time warp. A young girl with purple spiked hair and a nose ring sat chatting with a white haired woman in a fresh-from-church skirt and flowered blouse with a soft bow at the neck — perhaps her grandmother or a favorite neighbor. Farmers in seed-corn caps, middle-aged bleached blonde women with layered haircuts and too-small tank tops, and teenaged boys in logoed t-shirts filled the tables.

"I don't think there's anywhere to sit," Frannie whispered to Larry.

"You can sit here. I'm almost finished," a voice said behind them. They turned to see an older man sitting alone at a table for six.

"Are you sure?" Larry said.

The man smiled. "Wouldn't mind a little company, anyway."

Ben found an extra chair at another table, pulled it over, and they all sat. The next few minutes they perused the menus and made their choices. They looked around for a waiter.

"Name's Gus Riley, by the way. You have to go up to the window to place your order," the man said.

"Thanks," Mickey said and introduced the group. The women made their selections off the menu and their husbands got up to order.

Frannie turned to their host. "Thank you so much for sharing. Is the food good here?"

"The best," he answered. "You're not from town, I take it?"

She shook her head. "No, we're camping out at the park."

He frowned. "Been kind of strange goings on out there lately."

"You're right about that," Frannie said. "Did you know Mr. Leslie?"

"As well as I wanted to. Sorry, I know you ain't 'sposed to speak ill of the dead but he was a piece of work. Anybody in town'll tell you that. He'd do anything to keep his kids from having to take responsibility for any trouble they caused."

"Did they get in trouble a lot?" Jane Ann said.

Gus sat back in his chair and swirled the dregs of the coffee left in his mug, staring into it.

"Nuthin' serious—the girls that is. A little shoplifting, I think. The younger one had some mental problems, I guess. Don't know what happened to her. But Zach, he's another story." He shook his head. "Old Frank covered up for him all the time. One time, he and his friends filled the principal's office with garbage and old Frank swore Zach and his buddies was with him the whole time. And the Brian Murray thing—Frank alibied for Zach then, too, and the sheriff could never charge him or his friends."

Frannie said, "Doesn't sound like Zach had any reason to kill his dad, then."

Gus's head snapped up. "Killed him? Naw, Zach didn't do it. Worthless as he is, he didn't do that."

Ben and Larry returned to the table and Frannie changed the subject.

"This place been here a long time?"

"Oh, yeah. Wasn't always Chinese though. Mexican for a while, and before that just a diner. Always sold gifts though." Gus scraped back his chair and stood up. "Nice to meet you all. Gotta get going. Enjoy your meal." He tipped his hat and was gone.

Frannie and Ben went to get plates and plastic tableware while Nancy and Mickey filled drink cups. Their order was called and a flurry of chaos ensued as the ubiquitous white cartons with red pagodas and Chinese lettering were handed around, examined, and passed on to the proper diner. Jane Ann filled the men in on Gus Riley's opinion of Frank Leslie and his murder.

"People weren't very happy about not getting their race awards yet," Nancy commented.

"Yeah," Mickey laughed. "But they didn't complain too loud because it would look bad."

"I'm sure the ice cream helps," Ben said.

Frannie was hungrier than she realized and devoured her pork-fried rice with gusto. A few tastes were shared back and forth across the table. She decided against ordering ice cream afterwards and felt pretty smug about that.

BACK AT THE campground, Frannie was only too happy to slip off her socks and shoes and kick back in her reclining lawn chair with a book. Larry and Mickey had gone into the camper, Ben and Nancy for a walk, and Jane Ann was buried in her own book.

The day had turned out beautiful. A soft breeze rustled the leaves in the tops of the trees and kept the temperature comfortable while the sun made her drowsy. It was quiet because many of the campers had left, facing school and work on Monday.

So she had almost dozed off when she heard footsteps and a quiet voice.

"Ms. Shoemaker?"

She jumped a little and opened her eyes to see Odee Lumley walking toward her from the road, Peaches on a bright pink leash. Jane Ann had apparently gone in so she was alone in the campsite.

Frannie sat forward, closing her book. "Odee, how are you doing?"

Odee's friendly, round face crumpled as she fought back tears.

"I came to apologize for being so rude this morning."

"Oh, no, I don't blame you at all." Frannie pulled a lawn chair around next to her. "Have a seat, please."

Odee sat down and pulled Peaches up in her lap, but couldn't quite collect herself enough to talk so Frannie went on.

"Darius told Larry yesterday about his meeting with Frank Leslie, and even though he's not an active police officer any more, he felt obligated to report it. I'm really sorry."

"I understand," Odee said, back in control. "I know that Darius would not have harmed anyone, but *you* don't really know us and of course your husband has to do his duty." She gave her slow, sweet smile. Frannie doubted that she could be as gracious if the situation was reversed.

"So now what? What did the sheriff say?"

"He just said we couldn't leave since Darius had a motive and opportunity. But he didn't do it." She was calm now and very matter-of-fact.

"There seems to be...," Frannie hesitated, not sure how much she should say. Oh, what the hell. "...a lot of people tied together in this thing. Several old grudges and a previous unsolved murder. And there was the shooting last night." She watched Odee's face but there was no flicker of guilt or anything. And what connection between Darius and Zach Leslie could there possibly be anyway?

Without meaning to, Odee answered that question. "Darius thought that maybe Mr. Leslie's son might recognize our claim on the land. But why would he, if the money actually went to some scam artist? I told him it was hopeless."

"So, how will this loss affect you? Obviously, it's not good but—and it's none of my business, I know—you didn't have to mortgage your home or anything to make this investment, did you?"

Odee shook her head. "It was money Darius inherited. It just will make it very difficult to have any frills in our retirement—travel, a better camper, things like that."

"I'm really sorry," Frannie repeated. "Maybe if you give the sheriff all the info you have, they will eventually track down the scammer."

"That would be nice, but I'm not going to get my hopes up. It's too easy for someone to disappear over the Internet." She sighed. "Let's talk about something else. Do you have children?"

They spent the next quarter hour describing their families and agreeing on the joys of grandchildren. Odee put Peaches on the ground and got up.

"We'd better finish our walk and get back. Darius will think something dire happened to us, too."

Impetuously, Frannie said, "Why don't you join us for supper this evening? We're going to go to the decathlon awards ceremony later, but my brother-in-law, Mickey, is going to do a shrimp boil for supper. And he always cooks enough for the whole campground."

"Really?" Odee said. "That would be wonderful. My uncle in South Carolina used to make that for family gatherings. I was going to have to find a grocery store to get something for supper."

"Mickey does it well and we'd love to have you. I'll let you know a time when we get back from the ceremony."

"Okay. See you later." Her glow removed any reservations Frannie had about issuing the invitation without consulting the others.

HER NEED FOR a nap had passed and she was well into her book when the sheriff's car pulled up.

He strode toward her, took the chair Odee had vacated, removed his hat, and wiped his brow with a snowy white handkerchief. He wasn't smiling.

"Mrs. Shoemaker, I'm starting to wonder why you are smack in the middle of everything that's been happening this weekend." He stared at her and waited for an explanation.

Frannie bristled at his innuendo. "Good afternoon to you, too, Sheriff. And I don't know — except that this isn't a huge place. You're the one who brought us into it."

"But it makes me wonder if you weren't involved earlier," he said.

Frannie sat bolt upright. "Us? What motive could we possibly have had?"

He ignored that. "How do I know it wasn't you who found the turtle and either witnessed or committed the crime? You claim to have found a shoe that wasn't there. You were at the old church last night when Zach Leslie was shot. Maybe you even made the call to get him there. And you were on the trail today where Normadean was pushed."

"She was pushed?" Maybe Mark Masters was right.

"Or fell." He looked uncomfortable at his slip.

"That's all coincidental. We never heard of Frank Leslie before this weekend. None of us have any reason to hurt Normadean or Zach Leslie."

"I don't like coincidences. You're hiding something. Your husband keeps trying to shut you up."

Frannie threw up her hands. "*Only* because he was a cop and he doesn't want me interfering in police business."

This was nuts. She had just tried to reassure Odee about the sheriff's suspicions and now she and her friends seem to have become his focus. She started to protest more just as Larry emerged from the camper.

"Good afternoon, Sheriff."

"Larry, the sheriff seems to think one of us is the murderer."

Her husband stopped and looked at the sheriff, speechless for a moment.

"I didn't say that." The sheriff put up his hands in protest.

"It certainly sounded like it," Frannie said.

"What *did* you say, Sheriff?" Larry said.

The sheriff shrugged, less hostile than he had been with Frannie. "I'm just asking myself why you people have been involved with every attack and odd event this weekend. Just looking for an explanation."

Larry stared at the sheriff, deciding what to say, but Frannie barged ahead.

"What about Zach Leslie? What about the ethanol protesters? What about Normadean?"

Sheriff Jackson raised one eyebrow. "What about Normadean?"

"I don't know," Frannie admitted. "But I think Normadean was involved in the incident with Zach last night."

"Why?" He leaned forward in his chair.

She explained about the note on Normadean's clipboard. "I know Normadean suspects Zach in her cousin's murder, which would give her a good reason to hurt him. Maybe that incident had nothing to do with Frank's murder. Maybe her fall today didn't either. One of the protesters and one of Zach's friends got into it while we were waiting. That Mark Masters and a guy named Cory—or Cody—Stanley. Something like that. They were both in the race."

"A fight?" the sheriff asked.

"Just verbal. Other people calmed them down."

"What did you do with this alleged note?"

Frannie ignored the jab. "I gave the clipboard to the man who walked by after the last runners to tell us we were done. He was one of the officials."

The sheriff sighed. "Great. Let's hope so."

Larry interrupted. "Let's get back to your accusations, Sheriff. Your suspicions of us are based entirely on circumstantial evidence."

"I know that but, as I just explained to your wife, I don't like coincidences and this case is full of them."

Frannie jumped in again. "What about the geocaching log? Were you able to find out who the last signer was?"

"I can't divulge that. And, as you said, the person who found the turtle and dropped it may not have signed the log." There was no question who he thought that person or persons might be.

Frannie gave up and took another tack. "How is Normadean? Is she still in the hospital?"

"Sprained ankle. She's home—insists she's going to run this award ceremony this evening. So," the sheriff looked from one to the other. "You're kind of buddies with this Darius Lumley and his wife. Did you know them before this weekend?"

"No!" Larry was getting angry. "I told you last night about him meeting Frank Leslie. Why would I do that if we were close friends?"

"I wouldn't know." His disdain seemed to say he couldn't be expected to understand their kind of friendship. He took out a notebook. "I should have done this earlier. I'm gonna need your names, addresses and phone numbers. Your friends, too."

Frannie and Larry looked at each other, their mouths open.

"Yeah, sure," Larry said, resigned, and recited his name and contact information. Frannie did the same.

"Now I need your friends."

Frannie got up. "I'll get Jane Ann and Mickey."

Larry went to get Ben and Nancy.

When they returned, their bewildered friends gave the sheriff their own vital information.

"What's going on, Sheriff?" Ben asked when they were done.

"Just tying up some loose ends—filling in blanks—whatever." He got up and put his notebook in his pocket. "I'll remind you not to leave the area until I tell you that you can."

In stunned silence, they watched him walk away.

CHAPTER TWENTY ONE
SUNDAY MID-AFTERNOON

NANCY TURNED TO Frannie and Larry.

"What was that about?"

"He's added us to his suspect list," Frannie said.

"What?" Mickey said.

Larry pulled a water bottle out of the cooler. "We've been mixed up in everything that's happened. I'm not so sure he actually suspects us. He may be just covering his butt in case one of us is actually involved."

They started talking at once. Larry tried to explain the sheriff's point of view.

"Do we need to contact our lawyer, Larry?" Nancy asked.

"Not at this point. I think he's just blowing smoke."

Frannie said, "Before he stopped, Odee had just been here to apologize for ignoring us this morning. I felt so sorry for her, I invited them to join us tonight for the shrimp boil. Will that work, Mickey?"

"I don't see a problem with that. We'll have plenty."

Frannie sighed with relief. "Good."

Larry looked at his watch. "What time is the big ceremony?"

"7:00, I think." She got up. "And I need to go take a shower."

WHEN SHE RETURNED, she hung her towel on the drying rack mounted on the back of the camper. She ran her fingers through her wet curls and looked around the area. Mickey was at the end of his motorhome putting together the turkey fryer that he would use for the shrimp boil.

"Hey, Mick."

He looked up and grinned. "Are you clean finally?"

"Funny guy. So has anybody talked about finding any more caches?"

"No—I think everyone's in shock over the sheriff's visit. Were there any left in the park that we hadn't found?"

"A few nanos. Maybe they were mislabeled. Do you need any help here? Otherwise, think I'll go check the list."

Mickey flexed his muscles. "Help? Help! I am self-sufficient unto my own needs and those of others. I am —"

"Okay, okay. Enough already. I get the picture." She gave a weak laugh and went into the camper.

Larry was snoozing in his chair so she pulled up the list again for the area geocaches. One of the nanos was near the campground, on a trail on the side away from the lake. She grabbed a water bottle and put the coordinates into her Garmin.

Outside again, she said to Jane Ann. "I'm going to look for one of the nanos. Want to go?"

Jane Ann put down her book. "Sure."

171

"What about Ben and Nancy?"

"They left a little bit ago to see if the museum was open. You were at the shower."

"Okay — this one looks pretty close to the campground." Frannie pointed off in the direction indicated by the map.

"Better take your phone in case you fall in the lake or off a cliff," Mickey said.

"It's not by the lake."

"Still."

Frannie waved him off and glanced down at the Garmin to get the directions. It was the nicest day since they arrived. They headed down the road past the Lumleys' site. The trail was marked by one of the hiker silhouette signs and led down from the campground and away from the lake.

"We'd better watch our time — we only have about an hour," Jane Ann said.

Frannie scoffed. "Have you ever known me to miss supper?"

"Only when you've been abducted or are in the emergency room."

"Very funny."

As they descended the trail, the slight breeze turned the dappled sunlight to liquid, creating an underwater feeling. They had been to Dolomite several times but never been on this trail. The new territory combined with the lovely day to lift their spirits and lessen the worry over the murder case and the sheriff's accusations.

But the worry didn't completely go away. "Larry doesn't seem too concerned about the sheriff calling us suspects," Jane Ann said.

"I think it's wishful thinking," Frannie said. "I hope I'm wrong."

"He's not usually an optimist," Jane Ann said.

"True. Let's think about something else. This is a beautiful little ravine."

The trail snaked down the hill with several hairpin turns, which kept the slope gentle enough to make it easy walking. After the third turn, a stone structure appeared through the trees. As they got closer, they could see that it was a little bridge over a small ravine, built with a graceful arch and looking like something out of *The Hobbit*. Frannie checked the Garmin.

"Ten feet. The cache must be somewhere around that bridge."

"Isn't that the cutest thing?" Jane Ann said, and she paused to snap a photo.

The thickness of the shrubs around the bridge abutments created pockets of dark shadows contrasting to the bright yellow-green leaves. Many 'nano' caches were tiny magnetic containers, but there didn't appear to be any metal in the area to attach one of those to.

They walked back and forth on the bridge, examining the stone walls and looking for a gap where a cache could be hidden. Nothing. Frannie stepped off the far end and edged down the bank around the abutment. The undergrowth was quite thick and provided a multitude of hiding places, none of which yielded any treasures.

She worked her way under the bridge with no luck either.

Jane Ann walked down the other side." There's a few loose stones on this side," she said.

Frannie came up to that side from under the bridge. They were testing those stones without luck when they heard footsteps on the bridge.

Frannie flashed back to her childhood and whispered, "Who's that tromping over my bridge?" bringing a snicker from Jane Ann. The steps halted at the end of the bridge above them and then returned to the other end. The person retraced this path a couple of times and Frannie was starting to feel self-conscious about not calling out a greeting right away. Sounds of someone rustling and sliding down the slope came from the other side of the abutment and that was creeping her out.

Jane Ann finally called out "Hello?" The noises stopped and the quiet was more frightening than the sounds had been.

A branch snapped and a voice said, "Who's there?"

Frannie took a deep breath, chided herself for being so skittish, and stepped back under the bridge to the other side.

"Just us," she said, knowing how stupid that sounded.

It was the young man from the teardrop trailer. Site #37. bmyers. Well, she didn't know that for sure, but in his hand he held a Garmin similar to hers. So it seemed like a safe bet that he was the person who had signed the log and dropped the turtle on Frank Leslie's body. She didn't think he was the killer—there were too many others with motives. She hoped he wasn't, anyway.

"Oh, hi!" he said. "The lady who does geocaching." He shifted and looked at the Garmin in his hand like he had never seen it before. "Um, it sounded interesting so I looked it up and decided to try it."

Jane Ann emerged from under the bridge and the young man gave her a startled look. Frannie wondered if he expected her to be alone, but she said, "Obviously, we're looking for the same one you are, but we haven't had much luck yet."

He gathered himself and stood straighter. "How do you know what you're looking for?" He either *was* new at this or a good actor.

"Well, this one said it's a nano, which means it's very small. But sometimes they get changed out and not updated on the website." She explained about the Ninja turtles, watching his face as she talked. He didn't flinch.

"We've found most of the others in the park but are still missing one turtle." Jane Ann explained about the trackables. "If this one really is a nano, a turtle wouldn't fit in it, so we was hoping it had been changed."

"Can I help? You can log it if we find it; I just want to see how this works."

"Sure. We've already searched this side and we were just looking at the other side." Frannie glanced at her watch. "We only have about twenty more minutes and then we need to head back." They led him around to the other side and showed him the loose stones they had been working at.

Despite Frannie's conviction that he was not dangerous, she kept him in her line of sight. A couple of offhand comments made her more sure that he was *not* new at geocaching. He was hiding something.

The loose stones did not conceal any caches, so Frannie backed up from the bridge, examining the ground and shrubs for hiding places. Jane Ann went back to the top of the bridge, searching the weeds and shrubs framing the end.

"Hey—" Frannie wasn't sure what to call him, so she said, "I'm Frannie, by the way. And you are?"

"Paul. Paul Myers. Nice to meet you, officially that is." He had a pleasant smile.

So not a 'B' initial. Still, she was suspicious.

"You, too. That's my sister-in-law, Jane Ann. Well, Paul, look over here, where they dumped the extra rock when they built the bridge." He sidestepped down the slope to where she pointed.

"See how most of the rocks have sunk into the bank over the years? But here's one that's been put back recently." She reached down, brushed some leaves away, and gently pulled the rock out. There underneath, rested a small metal container but not small enough to be a nano.

"This might be it," she said.

Jane Ann peered over the bridge parapet. "Did you find something?

Frannie held up the container. She stood up and unclipped the top. Inside, a small notebook served as the log, and under that was a green plastic figure with a tag. "Yes!" she said, pumping her fist in the air.

"Woohoo!"said Jane Ann.

"Wow. That's great. So you found four of these now?" Paul Myers pointed to the turtle.

"Well, three actually. The other one was just found in the woods, no longer in the cache. It was near the site of that murder. The police are trying to track who found it through the website." Frannie watched his face closely. Behind his head a few bugs flitted in a beam of sunlight and the woods were quiet.

"Oh. Really? Do they think it had something to do with the murder?"

"I guess maybe the person who dropped it might be a witness." Standing further down the bank from Paul, she had a good view of his shoes. Hiking shoes. Like the one she had found on the rocks behind the CCC Museum. She straightened up and looked at her watch again. "We've got to get going! Thanks for your help." She waited for him to move out of the way so she could get back to the bridge.

"I didn't do much." He held out his hand. "Do you need help getting back up?"

She put her hands behind her back. Silly. But still. "No, I'll be fine. You are in my way, though." She smiled and hoped she exuded confidence.

"Oh. Sorry." He turned and scrambled up the bank and she followed. He waved them ahead of him on across the one lane bridge. Frannie didn't like turning her back on him—just as a precaution—but there didn't seem any graceful way to avoid it. Larry would say that graceful shouldn't come into it, but she reasoned that if he was guilty of something and they acted suspicious of him, she would be even less safe. So they scooted on across the bridge, Frannie looking at her watch again to reinforce the impression of her demanding schedule. And that somebody might come looking for them if they didn't show up on time. She could hear him plodding behind them, not fast but steady, and resisted the temptation to look back.

A knot of uncertainty replaced the carefree mood they had enjoyed on the walk down to the bridge. Frannie wasn't really afraid but felt she needed to stay alert.

They reached the main road that circled the campground without incident and Paul Myers took his leave to head back to his site.

"Check out his shoes," Frannie said, when Myers was out of earshot.

"His shoes? Why — ?" Jane Ann paused and then said, "Oh, I get it. The one you found on the rocks, right?"

"Or just like it," Frannie said.

Larry had been talking to Bob from across the road and met them as they walked back.

"Been meeting strange guys?"

"Right. George Clooney couldn't make it. That was his stand-in."

"George must not pay well."

She made a face at him. "He isn't *that* bad. I think you're jealous."

They returned to the circle in their own campsite.

Jane Ann prodded her. "Show 'em what you found."

Frannie felt the bulge in her pocket and pulled out the turtle. "Oh, Larry, look!"

He turned toward her and broke into a grin. "You found it. Good going."

Ben and Nancy had joined them and Frannie brandished the turtle. She described the find.

"Who was that guy really? Besides George Clooney's stand-in," Larry said.

"He has that little teardrop camper over in the outside row. His name is Paul Myers and he lives nearby."

"Myers?" Nancy's eyebrows went up.

Frannie nodded. "The guy in site #37."

Larry looked from one to the other. "What are you ladies talking about?"

"Remember the piece of log we found and gave the sheriff?" Frannie said.

"With a considerable amount of time in between those two events as I recall," Larry said. "Hence probably one of the reasons we're under suspicion."

Frannie ignored this. "The user name of the last person who found the cache and signed the log was 'bmyers.' Nancy and I noticed the name Myers on site #37 but turns out his first name is Paul."

"You don't sound convinced that he is not 'bmyers' though," Larry said.

"I don't know. I visited with him one day when I was coming back from the shower house. I told him we were doing some geocaching and he acted like he'd never heard of it."

"Maybe he hadn't," Nancy said.

"Maybe. But he arrived at the location today shortly after we did. He asked questions, but made a couple of comments that made him sound like he had experience. And his Garmin didn't look new. Besides, he was wearing hiking boots that were just like the one we found behind the CCC Museum."

CHAPTER TWENTY-TWO
SUNDAY LATE AFTERNOON

LARRY THOUGHT ABOUT that a minute and looked toward the road where he had seen the young man follow Frannie out of the woods.

"The b could mean something else. Or maybe 'pmyers' was already taken."

"Well, the sheriff was going to find out from the website who the person was. But when I asked him earlier this afternoon, he wouldn't tell me if he found out."

"Wise move on his part."

She stuck out her tongue at him. "Anyway, I figure if he didn't get a name, he would have told me that."

He rubbed the back of her neck. "I love your logic. Are we contributing anything to supper?"

"I have rolls I'm going to try and bake on the fire."

"Those rosemary ones? Great!"

"How's the boil coming?" Frannie said to Mickey.

"I've been chopping my fingers to the bone."

"Eww, that's disgusting."

"Well, not my fingers, but potatoes, onions, sausage, carrots. It will just take a half hour or so once we get the water boiling. I'll have to sample the beer first—make sure it's the right flavor."

"Of course."

The men plugged in the turkey fryer and Mickey added a can of beer and seasoning to the water. He opened another can and sat down to wait for the water to come to a boil.

"A watched pot. . ." Larry said.

"Shut up," Mickey said.

"Not to interrupt this scintillating conversation, but I need to go tell Lumleys what time we're eating. What do you think, Mickey?" Frannie got up from her chair.

"About an hour."

"I thought you said it would only take a half hour?"

"I meant a half hour after the water boils."

"Good thing you're such a good cook because it requires an awful lot of patience to be the recipient of those meals. I'll see if they want to come up for drinks beforehand. C'mon, Cuba. Let's go for a walk and see Peaches."

Cuba looked as if she was not as enamored of Peaches as her mistress but she couldn't resist the word "walk." She played it cool, though, and stretched for a long minute before succumbing to her leash. On the way to the Lumleys, she trotted briskly with frequent stops to check the fragrance of an electrical post or examine a dead bug.

Odee and Darius were sitting in their lawn chairs. Conversation was sparse as Odee leafed through a magazine and Darius read a paperback. The atmosphere was not cheerful.

"Hi!" Frannie called, hoping not to startle them.

Odee turned in her chair. "Oh! Great to see you." Frannie sensed that she had been trying to keep Darius' spirits up and was exhausted from the strain.

"You too. Just wanted to tell you that we will be eating in about an hour, but you're welcome to come up any time and we can visit."

"What can we bring?" Odee asked.

"Just your preference of beverage. Believe me, when Mickey cooks, he empties grocery shelves."

Darius laughed and said they'd be up in a few minutes. Frannie continued around the campground with the dog. There was no sign of Paul Myers at Site #37.

BY THE TIME Frannie and Cuba returned to the campground, the Lumleys were seated in the circle, questioning Mickey about the boil. Frannie took Cuba off her leash and hooked the Lab to the regular tether before she went in the camper to prepare her rolls to bake.

She put the Dutch oven containing rolls topped with rosemary, sea salt and butter in the coals to cook. Mickey had cooked the potatoes and onions the required time and was adding the chunks of smoked sausage. Laughter rose with the campfire smoke as Larry and Ben harassed the cook.

The clatter of plastic plates and bowls added to the noise as Nancy set the table. Jane Ann arranged metal trays on another table to spread out the boil when it was done. Larry added the shrimp to the boil and Mickey announced "Four minutes."

When the shrimp was done. Mickey and Larry drained the broth off the boil and carried the fryer to the prepared table where they dumped the fragrant mix of shrimp, meat and vegetables. Frannie pulled the Dutch oven out of the fire and carefully lifted the golden rolls out of the pot and onto a plate.

After filling their plates, they seated themselves at the picnic table and raised their glasses in a toast.

Larry said, "May the sheriff release us all from his clutches."

Odee clinked her glass with the rest, but looked at Larry, puzzled. "What do you mean?"

"Apparently, we are now included on his list of suspects along with you," Frannie said.

Odee set her glass down. "You're kidding. Why?"

Larry salted his boil with vigor, earning a frown from his wife. "We've been in the middle of everything that's happened."

"But you don't have any motive," Darius said. "At least I have that land scam. I mean, not that I *want* to be a suspect, but I don't get why you would be."

"I think the sheriff just feels he can't ignore our connection to the case," Larry said.

"Frannie, you said that guy from Site #37 was wearing shoes like the one we saw on the rocks?" Jane Ann said.

"I'm sure of it."

"So why would he not come forward if he was a witness?" Ben said.

"Because he's the murderer?" Mickey said.

"Or because he's been threatened," Jane Ann added.

"That's a good point," Frannie said. "The whole thing with Zach, his sisters, Ed and Brian, Normadean—so many old grudges. Just seems like it has to be connected."

"If Zach killed his father, I wonder why they were out in the woods in the first place." Jane Ann got up with her bowl. "I need more of that stuff."

"Yeah, Zach doesn't look like he's into long walks in the country," Ben said.

A phone played the theme from *The Muppet Show,* and Odee smiled shyly as she pulled hers out of her pocket. She got up from the table and walked away, reassuring the caller in low tones. When she returned, she said to Darius, "Ann." She explained to the others, "Our daughter. She has been so worried about her dad."

"It's much harder to prove you didn't do something than to prove you did," Darius observed. But he didn't seem nearly as worried as Odee was.

"Nancy and I have to be back to work by Tuesday," Ben said. "The sheriff better get this cleared up soon."

Mickey stood up. "If everyone's done. I'm going to clear up this mess before we go to the awards thing." Jane Ann got up to help.

"Is anyone in our group getting a prize?" Frannie looked at Nancy and Ben.

"Ben should," Nancy said, "and Jane Ann might for her age group."

"Ah. Don't let her hear you say that!"

CHAPTER TWENTY-THREE
SUNDAY EARLY EVENING

THE AWARDS WERE being given at the same pavilion where the runners registered. A small podium stood on one end of a picnic table and a box of medals trailing red, white and blue ribbons sat next to it. The other tables were nearly full and a few people romped around outside, enjoying the weather and throwing Frisbees.

Since there wasn't really any place left to sit, Frannie and Larry moved outside the pavilion under the trees. Mickey joined them, while Ben, Nancy, and Jane Ann visited with some of the other runners. Mickey and Larry discussed the shrimp boil and Frannie leaned against a tree.

She spotted Zach Leslie hobbling up on his crutches and saw him jerk his head toward a nearby old oak. Following his line of sight, it seemed he was signaling to the Cody-or-Cory guy from the obstacle race. Once Leslie and his buddy met behind the huge tree, Frannie ambled over that way.

Loud whispers from the other side of the tree pulled her in closer.

"What the hell was your dad doing with that knife?"

"What do you care? Only his fingerprints are on it."

"But if they link it to that little creep Brian, they're going to wonder why your dad had it."

"Maybe they'll think he did it."

"You're crazy. And now you'll take off and the rest of us have to deal with the fallout."

"Shut up about it. Got it? Just shut up about it." Zach Leslie tottered around the tree trunk and headed for the pavilion. He glanced sideways and caught Frannie staring at him. She shut her mouth quickly and turned away, moving toward Larry, but not before she caught a glare from Zach so malevolent that she shuddered. Larry looked down at her when she took his arm.

"What?"

"Can't a wife take her husband's arm?"

"When you're the wife, there's usually something behind it." He grinned but patted her hand and left it curled around his arm.

"I'll tell you later." Frannie stole a look in the direction Zach had gone and found him leaning against a pole on the other side of the shelter, still staring at her.

The clatter of conversation in the shelter became more focused and people turned toward the parking area. Normadean, guided by her cousin Ed, walked much the same as Zach only using a cane, followed by a couple of volunteers. She gave a vigorous wave to rally her troops and assure them that she would not fail them.

When the procession got to the shelter, Normadean handed her cane to Ed and leaned on the podium. She was recovered enough to give directions to several people at once. Underlings flurried around, moving the box of awards, handing her the clipboard and producing a hand-held mike.

Frannie craned her neck around and saw Zach's friend, Cody Stanley, walk out from behind the old oak in the direction of the road. He got in a car and drove away. She stole a glance at Zach, but he wasn't standing by the post any more.

Normadean blew a whistle for attention. An immediate silence settled over the shelter.

"Thank you for coming tonight and for participating or volunteering in our fundraiser. I apologize that this was postponed because of my—uh— accident, but as a reward, there will be treats. With donations and entry fees, we have raised over $4000 for our beautiful park." She paused to allow the cheers she expected.

She raised her hand for attention, as effective as the whistle. "We had 137 people participate in the various events and," she referred to her clipboard, "68 volunteers. Thank you again."

Applause this time underlined her thanks.

"We'll give out the awards first for the archery contest." Frannie tuned out while Normadean read name after name in age group after age group. She applauded absently for each recipient as Normadean went on to the logrolling contest and other competitions. Mark Masters was in the crowd and got medals for the obstacle course and the bike race. The 5K race was last and Ben got third place. Nancy also medaled, and as predicted, Jane Ann placed in the over 60 group. She brandished her medal as if it was Olympic gold.

"I can't wait to show Justine," she said. "I always told her she takes after me." Justine, Jane Ann and Mickey's daughter, had been a state track champion in high school. The others might have agreed with Jane Ann's claim if Justine hadn't been adopted.

"That will convince her, dear," Mickey said. "Congratulations."

Jane Ann swung the medal by its red, white and blue ribbon. "Anyway, I'm going to hang this from the dining room chandelier at home."

While Normadean was finishing the awards, a van pulled up to the edge of the parking lot. The driver opened the back, rolled out a small freezer, and proceeded to push it up toward the shelter. A young boy followed with a cardboard box.

"Perfect timing," Normadean shouted. "To wrap up our great weekend, we have free ice cream sundaes." She paused while the crowd quieted again. "This is our locally made Zweigler ice cream — the best you'll ever taste! Give these guys a few minutes to set up and then come and get it!"

While they waited, Frannie told Larry about the conversation she had overheard between Zach and his buddy.

"Oh, that's why you got so affectionate all of a sudden," Larry said. "It does sound like they had some complicity in that earlier murder. But doesn't prove anything about Frank Leslie."

And for Larry, that was admitting a lot.

Frannie watched the crowd. She still did not see Zach Leslie, but noticed Paul Meyers nearby headed toward the ice cream line.

"Hi, Paul!" she called out.

He turned and acknowledged her with a little wave. Then he quickly glanced toward Normadean, whose attention had been caught by Frannie's shout, and, changing direction, made a beeline for the parking lot.

"That was odd," Larry said, watching him go.

"You're telling me," Frannie said. "And Normadean seems awfully interested."

The group got in the ice cream line. Normadean watched Frannie closely but kept up a conversation with one of the medal winners.

When they got even with Normadean, she leaned over to Frannie and said, "Can I talk to you a minute?"

Frannie said "Sure," and as she stepped out of line, said to Larry, "Butterscotch and nuts."

"Gotcha," he said.

"I just wanted to thank you for all your help this morning after my accident and taking care of that race." Normadean raised her eyes to the sky and put her hand on her chest. "If you hadn't documented their order and gotten it all going again, the whole thing would have been for *nothing*!"

Frannie smiled. "I'm sure people would have understood. After all, it's for a good cause."

"Oh, yes, of course, but some of these runners are, you know, *fanatics*. Anyway, you made it possible for this ceremony to go ahead. I have a gift for you and your friends."

"That's not necessary at all," Frannie said.

"I know, I know, but I want to. Can you come to the park office after this?"

"I'll check with my husband. I think he wanted to go to town and gas up the truck tonight because we're leaving early tomorrow." She didn't add *If the sheriff lets us.*

"Well, I can stop by tomorrow—although I have an early doctor appointment...Tell you what. Why don't you just ride over with me? I have a few things to put away and then I'll give you a ride back to your camper."

"I'll see," Frannie said. "How is your ankle?"

Normadean shifted on her cane. "It's going to be fine. They made too big of a fuss."

"Better safe than sorry," Frannie said.

"I just don't have time for it. But, what's done is done."

Larry came back with a cup of ice cream dripping with butterscotch and nut topping.

"Larry, Normadean wants me to stop at the park office for something after this. Do we have time?"

Larry looked at his watch. "Not really. Mickey just told me the gas station closes at 8:30. Can we stop on the way back?"

"I won't be there that long," Normadean said firmly.

"Maybe Ben and Nancy could make the stop—?" Frannie asked.

191

Larry was shaking his head. "Mickey and Jane Ann just left with them. They're going to clean up the turkey fryer."

"So come with me." Normadean looked at Frannie."I'll bring you back to the campground. Your group really helped me out today and I have thank you gifts for all of you."

Larry looked at Frannie. "What do you want to do?"

"That's fine."

"Or I can pick you up on my way back, but I don't want you to be waiting alone, so—"

"It'll be fine," Frannie said again. "Normadean can take me back." She was still convinced of Normadean's involvement in the attack on Zach Leslie but knew the motive was very personal. That didn't justify it, but didn't feel like a threat either.

Chapter Twenty-Four

Sunday Night

FRANNIE FOLLOWED NORMADEAN to her car. The park office was in a small utilitarian building near the entrance.

"The park lets the Friends group have a little office space here," Normadean said as she balanced with her cane and unlocked the door. She hit a switch to the side and florescent lights revealed a typical plain office space with two desks, several file cabinets, and a computer. A short counter separated the work area from the entrance and offered brochures about area points of interest. Normadean went to another door on the left side and opened it, turning on more lights. The tiny room held a table, chair, bookshelves, and one filing cabinet.

"Just put that on the table," Normadean said, indicating the box of awards and supplies that Frannie had carried in for her.

Normadean went to the shelves and pulled a large white sheet off each of three different stacks and laid them on the table beside the box. "There are three couples in your group, right?"

"Yes."

"These are prints of pen and ink drawings of the park done by a local artist. This one is the bathhouse of course,

193

this one the trail, and this one the spring. I want you each to have one — sorry they aren't framed."

"That's very thoughtful of you but you don't need to do that," Frannie said, lifting each one individually and examining it. She looked up at Normadean and smiled her thanks. The expression on the woman's face shocked her — worry and fear.

"Is something wrong?" Frannie said.

Normadean shook her head. "No, no. Just tired I guess. I think I'll put these things away in the morning. Are you ready to go?"

"Sure. I'll get the lights."

Back in the car, Normadean said, "The sheriff said your group is into that geocaching — is that what it's called?"

"Yes, we do some of that when we're camping. Why?"

"Do a lot of people do it? I mean do you share with others how to find these things?"

"Do you mean you want to know how to start?"

"Oh, no, I don't think so. I'm just curious. I mean, if you find one, do you tell others how to find it?"

"Absolutely not. Each person has to find it on their own."

Normadean kept her eyes on the dark road ahead. "So are there a lot of people in the park now who are doing it?"

"I don't know. I only saw one other person. Why?"

Again Normadean answered with her own question. "Was it that guy—Paul, I think—who was at the awards ceremony?"

So Normadean had been watching when Frannie tried to get Paul Myers attention, Frannie thought. But why?

"Yes, it was. How do you know him?"

"Um, he was in one of the events, I think, or maybe two." She was getting flustered and pretended to concentrate on her driving.

"But how did you know he was into geocaching?" Frannie persisted.

"Oh—I think I saw him when I was setting up a course or something. I didn't talk to him."

Frannie was quiet a moment. She remembered what Normadean had said to her cousin Ed in the bar. That Frank Leslie had tried to 'bury the evidence' but it didn't work. "Normadean, who do you think killed Frank Leslie? The sheriff thinks we're involved somehow but we definitely are not."

"What?" She started to swerve and cranked the wheel back quickly. Frannie grabbed the armrest. "*Me*? How would I know?" Normadean's voice was almost squeaky.

"I was just wondering. You know everyone around here—I thought maybe you had an idea." Frannie looked ahead, trying to appear unconcerned. "Here's the campground entrance up here."

"Yes, I *know*. I've spent a lot of time in this park."

"Of, course," Frannie said. "I wasn't thinking."

Normadean collected herself. "I'm sorry—didn't mean to snap at you. I really am tired, I guess." She gave Frannie a little apologetic smile as she pulled up to their campsite.

"I'm not surprised. You've had a very long day." Frannie opened the car door. "Thank you very much for the prints. It was nice meeting you. Good luck with your park projects."

"Park projects? Oh, sure—thank you." And she drove off almost before Frannie got the door closed.

LARRY WASN'T BACK yet but the others were gathered around the fire.

"Where's your hubby?" Mickey said.

"He went to town to gas up the truck." Frannie held out the prints. "Normadean wanted each of us to have one of these prints. For helping when she had her accident this morning."

Jane Ann took them and leafed through them. "How nice. These are cool."

"It was nice. But maybe it's a bribe. Of sorts," Frannie said.

Nancy raised her eyebrows and Ben said, "Why?"

"I asked her who she thought killed Frank and she nearly went off the road. Something's been bothering me that Normadean said when she was talking to Ed the other night in the bar."

"Yeah?" Mickey said.

"She said Frank tried to bury the evidence but that wasn't going to work. I thought she meant it figuratively, but what if she meant it literally?"

"What do you mean?" Jane Ann asked.

"The knife. What if Frank had the knife that killed Brian hidden on his farm all these years and now thought that if he was going to sell the farm, he'd better hide it somewhere else?" Frannie rubbed her forehead and looked at the rest of the group.

"Like in the park?" Ben said.

"Why not? Right across the road from him—who would ever look for it there? No one is likely to go digging in the middle of the woods. But if he left it on the farm and they excavated to build a big plant, it might be discovered." Frannie was silent for a moment, thinking.

Headlights raked across the campsite as Larry turned the truck in beside the camper. Once Larry joined the group, Frannie brought him up to date on Normadean and her latest theory.

Jane Ann said, "But if Normadean knew he had the knife, why didn't she just report him? Why follow him?"

"Maybe she didn't follow him. She laid out the cross-country course. It went right by where Frank was found."

"You mean it was an accident?" Jane Ann said.

"Well, I don't think it was planned." Frannie said.

Jane Ann twirled the medal that she wore around her neck.

"Pretty proud of that, huh, Sis?" Larry said.

"What? Oh, this thing? One more to add to the collection is all." She picked up her wine glass and sipped it, batting her eyelashes.

"Collection?" Larry said.

"She has a blue ribbon on the fridge at home from a fifth grade spelling bee and one of those plastic trophies they give to every kid who participates in t-ball," Mickey said.

"Yeah, I'd forgotten about those."

"Forgotten?" Jane Ann said. "I had to hear about all of *your* awards and trophies every time I turned around."

"He is a little overbearing," Frannie agreed.

Larry held up his hands. "Whoa. I'm not overbearing. I just state the facts, ma'am."

Jane Ann twirled the medal on its ribbon. "Well, I'm just saying that some of us participate and win and some of us just watch." Her smirk ended Larry's comeback.

"What about the guy in site #37, Paul Myers? He sure acted strange tonight at the ceremony when you tried to talk to him," Larry said to Frannie.

"Larry, he knows something — I'm sure of it. Can't we go talk to him? Maybe if no one else is around, he'll tell us what it is so we can get out of here tomorrow," Frannie said.

Larry looked at her and ran his hand over his head. "Okay," he said slowly. "But I'm going to call the sheriff and asked him to meet us there."

WHEN FRANNIE AND Larry arrived at site #37, Paul Myers sat slumped in a lawn chair staring into a small fire. He held a long stick in one hand that he used to stir the coals. As they entered his site, he looked up, startled and then frightened. The firelight exaggerated his features.

"What do you want?" His tone was belligerent.

"We just want to talk to you," Larry said. He sat on the picnic table bench and Frannie sat beside him.

"About what? I don't know anything."

A strange reaction, thought Frannie, if he really didn't.

"I think you do know something," Larry said. "About the murder in the woods Thursday."

"You were there," Frannie said.

"I didn't do anything."

"No, but you saw it. You were geocaching, weren't you?"

"I told you, I never heard of geocaching before you told me about it." He pulled back into his chair.

"I don't believe you," Frannie said. "You have a Garmin that looks well used. You know more than you pretend to."

Larry leaned forward, rested his elbows on his knees, and clasped his hands. "Here's the thing. A lot of people are under suspicion for this murder. Several of us are not allowed to go home until the sheriff has this solved or has at least eliminated us as suspects."

"I can't leave either," Paul said, anguish on his face.

"Oh, really? So we aren't the only ones who think you are lying?" Larry said.

"I'm not lying!"

Frannie looked him in the eyes. "Paul, did somebody threaten you? Why are you afraid to come forward?"

"What? What are you talking about?"

She had hit a nerve. She pointed at his hiking shoes. "Shortly after the murder occurred, although we didn't know about it yet, we were geocaching on the other side of the creek and saw one of your shoes on a rock pile. An hour or so later it was gone. What happened? How did it get there?"

Paul hung his head. "I can't."

Sheriff Jackson's car pulled up. If possible, Paul Myers' face turned another shade of pale.

"Good evening," the sheriff said, as he got out of his car. "Mr. Myers, are you ready to tell me what happened?"

"I wasn't there!"

"You signed the log. I've confirmed that with the geocaching site. I would like permission to search your camper and truck. I can get a warrant if you wish."

Paul Myers seemed completely shattered. Frannie saw him glance at the white plastic garbage bag hanging on the side of the teardrop camper. A glimpse of green was barely visible through the thin plastic.

"Whatever," he finally whispered and hung his head.

"Sheriff," Frannie said. "You might want to check the trash first."

He frowned at her but examined the bag on its hook. He got a camera and a plastic sheet from his car and spread the sheet on the ground. Before he removed the bag, he photographed it. Then he carefully poured the contents on the sheet. A few beer cans and water bottles were interspersed with take-out containers, paper plates, and tin cans. And peeking out from under a pot pie box was a green plastic Teenage Mutant Ninja Turtle.

He took a pencil from his pocket and pointed at the turtle. He raised his eyes to look at Paul Myers. "Can you explain this?"

Paul gave him a pleading look. "She knows where I live."

"Who?" The sheriff's voice was harsh.

"That woman—that Normadean person. She says she has access to the campground records. I have a son." His voice faded out.

The sheriff pulled out a walkie-talkie. "Give me your address and I will have someone at your house within a few minutes."

"He's not there right now—he's with my ex-wife."

"Okay. Then tell me what you saw. We will protect your son."

Paul Myers took a deep breath. "Okay," he said.

CHAPTER TWENTY-FIVE
LATE SUNDAY NIGHT AND MONDAY MORNING

FRANNIE HAD TO strain to hear Paul's words at first.

"I was looking for the geocache named 'Chocolate' that was hidden in those woods." He took a deep breath and paused so long that Frannie wondered if he would need to be prodded for each sentence. But finally he continued. "I found it and sat down on a fallen tree to sign the log. I heard a noise and realized that someone was digging down the hill from me. It's always kind of spooky in the woods anyway, but I thought maybe it was a park person doing some maintenance. I peeked around a tree to see—it's some old guy with a shovel." Another long pause. His eyes seemed unfocussed as he relived the event.

"Go on," said the sheriff, quietly.

"He's looking around like he's guilty of something. Then I notice off to the side that woman—Normadean—coming up on him. She's carrying a handful of orange flags and every so often sticks one in the ground. When she sees the old man, she starts walking as quietly as she can. He's got a knife stuck in his belt and she comes up behind him and grabs it. He whirls around and she yells something about he isn't going to get away with it again."

"Did either of them see you?" the sheriff asked.

Paul shook his head. "Not at first. They struggle over the knife and I hear him give a little scream. He keels over and she stands there with the bloody knife. She wipes the handle on her shirt and throws it away from her, into the brush."

"What did you do then?"

"Nothing. I was scared. But when she threw the knife, she looked up the hill and saw me. I was frozen to that log. I drop the container and the pencil and the paper while I try to think what to do. She comes up that hill like a steamroller. She knows me because I had talked to her earlier about the races. She tells me if I don't keep my mouth shut she would find my family and I would be sorry. That she could get my address from the campground records. And that the old guy was going to bury that knife to cover up for an old murder." He stopped and stared off in the distance.

"Then what?"

"I didn't think I was in danger so I told her we needed to get the guy help. She said it was too late, but I told her I was going to check anyway. I went down and took his pulse and she was right—he was gone."

"What happened to the tag on the turtle?" Larry said.

Paul sighed. "After I checked his pulse, I stood up and pulled out my phone. I still had the turtle in my other hand and when I turned to tell her I was going to call 911, she had a gun on me!" His eyes grew wide at the memory. "She repeated her threats to my family and grabbed the turtle tag. It broke off. Then she yelled at me to get out so I took off down the hill and waded across the creek. I think she wanted to use the tag to frame me, but I figured if I didn't log it online, no one would ever know."

"And after you crossed the creek, you lost your shoe in the rocks," Frannie said.

He nodded. "I didn't know if she was chasing me or not. She's crazy. So I kept going and came back later to get my shoe."

"Well, lock up your stuff," the sheriff said. "I'm taking you in for obstruction and what happens after that depends on your continued cooperation."

"But I didn't do anything!"

"Right, you didn't. You didn't report a murder. You didn't tell the truth about knowing anything. As a consequence, a number of people have been under suspicion, more people have worried about a murderer on the loose, and another person was shot." He pulled out his handcuffs. "You can either lock up your stuff, or we can leave it like this and I'll take you in now."

Paul held up his hands. "Okay. Okay."

While he closed and locked his trailer, put his chair away and put out the campfire, the sheriff called in an alert to pick up Normadean and rolled up the sheet with the trash.

"So, what about Zach Leslie and the Brian Murray murder?" Frannie asked.

"We'll find out if that knife *was* used in his murder and reopen the case."

"You may also want to look at Normadean for the attack on Zach last night," Larry said.

The sheriff nodded. "I apologize for any inconvenience to you folks but I had no choice. You're free to leave now. I still can't quite wrap my head around Normadean being behind this. I think she's probably had anger issues for a long time, very controlled though. She was close to her aunt Betty and must have channeled all of her anger into her volunteer work. I know I'm being an armchair psychologist here but that's my guess."

"We'll be going in the morning," Larry said. They said goodbye and the sheriff ushered Paul Myers into his car, reciting his Miranda rights.

AS THEY WALKED back to the campsite, Larry put his arm around Frannie and she leaned her head on his shoulder. A sliver of a moon played hide-and-seek with wispy clouds and the campground was quiet.

"I'm exhausted," she said. "This has been one long day."

Larry agreed. "I think we'll sleep well tonight. Maybe we should think about taking up a more restful hobby than camping—say, knife throwing or rock climbing."

"Don't say knife," she said.

The rest of the group, including the Lumleys, waited expectantly by the fire.

"Well?" Mickey said. "Don't keep us in suspense."

Frannie related the story with Larry filling in the holes and toning down the color commentary.

"You were right about Normadean," Jane Ann said.

"So we're all free to go?" Odee said.

Larry nodded. "I think the sheriff will be by in the morning to give us the official go ahead."

Odee breathed a big sigh of relief and squeezed her husband's hand. "We need to celebrate," she said. "I'm cooking breakfast for all of you. About 8:30?"

"That would be great," Ben said.

Nancy leaned forward in her chair. "But why would Normadean shoot Zach, if it she was the one who did it? I know she hated him but that's a little extreme."

"She must have been trying to force him to confess to the murder of her cousin. That's what this all has been about, anyway," Frannie said.

"How sad," Jane Ann said. "There's nothing worse than an old grudge."

"More than a grudge. There's been a lot of tragedy — whatever happened to Zach's sister to put her in an institution, Brian's death, Frank Leslie getting his daughter to break off her engagement. A lot of lives affected." Frannie said. "Well, I need to turn in. See you all in the morning."

FRANNIE SLEPT IN, an extremely unusual occurrence. When she rolled over and looked at her watch, a little alarmed by the brightness of the sun pushing through the blinds, she was surprised to see it was after 7:00. Larry was already up, another rare event.

Outside, it looked like it was going to be the best day they'd had all weekend.

"Figures," Mickey said. "Always happens the day we go home."

"At least we don't have to pack up in the rain," Jane Ann said, always the optimist.

They worked around their sites, putting away lawn chairs, tablecloths, patio torches and other paraphernalia until it was time to go to the Lumleys' for breakfast. Odee had an egg dish cooking in a large electric skillet on their utility table and Darius was frying bacon on a griddle over the fire. They refilled their coffee mugs and found seats at the picnic table.

The eggs were savory, the bacon crisp, and the warm cinnamon rolls that Darius had picked up in town fragrant and sweet. The mood reflected the release of tension over the events of the weekend. They were just finishing when the sheriff's car pulled up.

"Beautiful morning!" Sheriff Jackson called out as he emerged from the patrol car.

"That it is!" replied Darius.

"Wanted to thank you all for your help. Sorry about the suspect thing but I really didn't have any choice," Jackson said when he got to the table.

"It's understandable," Larry said.

Not to me, Frannie thought, but wisely kept her mouth shut.

The sheriff turned to Odee and Darius. "I'm afraid I can't do much about the land scam. It probably involves people who don't live anywhere near here. I did report it though."

Darius shock his head. "I know. It was an expensive lesson."

"Any word on Normadean?" Mickey said.

The sheriff smiled grimly. "They picked her up this morning in Minnesota, headed for the Canadian border."

"Did you find out if she also shot Zach?" Frannie asked.

"She's not talking, and neither is he. If he is responsible for Brian Murray's murder and that's why she shot him, he's not going to admit it. But I'm confident we can get that case settled too, before it's all over. Sorry I can't return your turtle thing but I'm afraid it's evidence for the time being."

"Don't worry about that," Ben said. "I think we can get it replaced and move them all on."

"Well, the sheriff said, scratching his head, "let's hope that they don't have to do so much actual crime fighting at their next location."

HAPPY CAMPER TIPS

Happy Camper Tip #1

Grilled Blue Cheese Burgers: In one pound of ground beef, mix in 1 tablespoon of crushed garlic and 2 tablespoon of finely chopped onion and 2 Tablespoons of finely chopped basil. Form into 4 balls. Press 1 oz of blue cheese (of course I use Maytag blue), then flatten into patties, (make sure the cheese stays inside) then grill over medium to low coals until done to the way you like them. Top them with red onion and tomato.

We serve it with fresh-from-the-garden cucumbers, tomatoes, red onion sliced thin then then add black olives and your favorite Italian dressing (we use the bottled Olive Garden Italian kind) mix together then let sit while the burgers cook.--Julie Biver

Happy Camper Tip #2

Shutter Uppers: like S'mores, except you toast a marshmallow and a chewy carmel then put it on a saltine — Marietta Dugan Hartley

Happy Camper Tip #3

Zucchini Parmesan Bread: Especially for those of us who live in the Midwest, one cannot have too many zucchini recipes.

In a bowl, combine 3 cups of flour (I use 1/2 whole wheat), 3 tablespoons grated Parmesan cheese, 1 teaspoon salt, and 1/2 teaspoon each of baking powder and baking soda. In another bowl, beat 2 eggs, 1 cup buttermilk, 1/3 cup sugar and 1/3 cup melted butter or margarine. Add to dry ingredients and stir until moistened. Fold in 1 cup shredded zucchini and 1 tablespoon grated onion.

Bake in a greased 9 x 5 loaf pan at 350 for 1 hour.

Happy Camper Tip #4

Dip and Conversation Extender: ideal for camping; good for discussing the suspects: 1 can refried beans, 1 pint sour cream, hot sauce of choice, 1 8 oz. pkg., shredded Monterrey Jack cheese with jalapeños. In a 1 quart casserole dish, layer beans, sour cream, and hot sauce, topped by cheese. Bake at 350 for 20 minutes or until lightly brown and bubbly. Keep warm during serving to facilitate dipping. Serve with taco or similarly sturdy chips. — Roger Scholes

Happy Camper Tip #5

Double Duty Prep: When planning a weekend trip I make breakfast burrito and spaghetti fixings a few days ahead of the trip and freeze in gallon size bags. When time to pack, those frozen bags go into the ice chest and cut down on the need for a lot of ice. Another plus with this idea is those frozen bags make for quick meals! — Pat Sonoff

Happy Camper Tip #6

Single skillet meals: We like to cook extensive meals and exotic dishes, but sometimes time and/or the weather doesn't permit. I keep a small and a large electric skillet in the camper because in those instances, I love one dish meals. Some of our favorites:

Hash brown omelet: Fry a few strips of bacon. Remove and crumble. Then fry frozen hash browns in the bacon fat, pour beaten eggs with choice of additives (mushrooms, onions, sun dried tomatoes, and my favorite—Greek seasoning), sprinkle with bacon pieces and cheese and cook until done.

Sausage skillet: Cut summer sausage into chunks and brown in skillet. Add bite-sized chunks of potatoes. Cook until potatoes are nearly done; thrown in a can of corn and roasted red peppers.

Happy Camper Tip #7

Travel Mode: Every Rver needs to develop a system for moving their rig without jumbling everything inside. When we pack up, a number of things go on the bed. We have a flat screen TV that is not attached to the wall because it's an older trailer, the gooseneck bedside lamps that we use because we don't like the overhead lights, and anything else loose on the night stands lays on the bed. Everything on the bathroom counter fits in the medicine cabinet. We have a storage footstool that sits up on the dinette bench when we travel and holds, besides scrapbooks and campground information, the wall clock and other loose items. Our silverware is in one of those picnic caddies. When we are stopped, it sits on the counter, and when we travel, it slips into a cupboard.

Happy Camper Tip #8

Laundry: If you have a few items that need washing, put them in a tote with tight -fitting lid. Add water and soap and set the tote in the bathtub or shower while you are on the road. The motion will agitate the clothes. Rinse when you arrive, and hang out to dry.

Happy Camper Tip #9

Easy Chocolate Fudge: Line 8 or 9 inch square baking pan with foil. Combine 12 oz. pkg. of semi-sweet chocolate morsels & sweetened condensed milk in medium, heavy duty saucepan. Warm over lowest heat, stirring until smooth. Remove from heat; stir in nuts & vanilla extract. Spread evenly into prepared pan. Refrigerate for 2 hours or until firm. Lift from pan; remove foil. Cut into 48 pieces. (I lift foil out of pan & turn it upside down on a cutting board & remove foil from fudge to cut it). — Linda Harmon

Happy Camper Tip #10

Pineapple Tea Loaf: 3 cups Bisquick, 1 cup sugar, 1 cup quick oats, 1/2 teaspoons. baking soda, 1 cup milk, 1 egg, 1 cup crushed pineapple (drained), 1 cup chopped walnuts, 1 teaspoons. vanilla,

Bake in large loaf pan or 9x13 pan @ 350* about an hour. Test by inserting a tooth pick. — Linda Harmon

Happy Camper Tip #11

Pecan Pie Muffins: 1 cup packed light brown sugar, 2/3 cup butter, softened, 1/2 cup all-purpose flour, 2 eggs beaten, 1 cup chopped pecans

Preheat oven to 350*. Grease & flour 18 mini muffin cups or line with paper muffin liners. In a medium bowl, stir together brown sugar, flour and pecans. In a separate bowl beat butter and eggs together until smooth, stir into dry ingredients just until combined. Spoon batter into prepared muffin cups. cups should be about 2/3 full.

Bake at 350* for 20 to 25 minutes. Cool on wire racks when done. — Linda Harmon

Happy Camper Tip #12

Crockpot Stuffed Bell Peppers: 6 green peppers (washed, topped & seeded), 1/8 teaspoons. black pepper, 1-1/2 lb. ground beef, 1/8 teaspoons. basil, 1 cup cooked rice, 1/2 cup ketchup, 1 small onion, chopped, 1-8 oz. can tomato sauce, 1 teaspoons. salt (w/ or w/o seasoning)

Brown beef in large skillet. Combine meat & next 6 ingredients. Stuff bell peppers. Arrange bell peppers in large crockpot. Peppers can be stacked. Pour tomato sauce over peppers. Cook on low 6-7 hours or on high for 3-4 hours.—Linda Harmon

Happy Camper Tip #13

Table It: Many RVs, especially older ones, come with a pretty utilitarian and boring laminate dinette table. I've seen some interesting redos—from simply covering the table with a vinyl tablecloth and stapling it underneath to painting a new design or adding a map, postcards or photos and finishing with epoxy to using a countertop refinishing kit.

Happy Camper Tip #14

Awnings: These great attachments extend the living space on your camper, especially on hot sunny days or rainy ones. But a constant issue is the wind, and many of us have had to replace awnings because of it. Tie downs help. Some times we use straps to anchor ours to the picnic table but then the table isn't completely under the awning. You can purchase awning anchors that screw into the ground and we have had good luck with so far. Recently I saw a suggestion to use five-gallon buckets of water. Light to take along but about forty pounds when filled. You may want to add a little oil to discourage mosquito breeding or refill frequently if you have pets but seems like a good idea.

Happy Camper Tip #15

Playing with Fire: Two common items you have around the house can be used to make fire and even sparklers. If you touch both terminals of a 9V battery to a wad of steel wool, it will immediately begin to burn and can be used to light kindling. Use the finest steel wool grade and pull it apart to get more oxygen in it. You can also stuff it in a wire whisk, tie a rope to the whisk, and swing it around for a sparkler effect. And it's environmentally friendly. — Amy Hardy

Happy Camper Tip #16

Crockpot potatoes: This recipe is not as high calorie as some potato dishes. Wash and slice six potatoes into the crockpot. Add 1/2 cup of water and a mix of one teaspoon each of salt, pepper, garlic powder, minced onion, Italian seasoning, and parsley plus 1/2 teaspoon of dill. Top with four tablespoons of butter (or a little less) and cook on low for 3-4 hours. Better double the whole thing.

Happy Camper Tip #17

The Sound of Music: If you want a musical accompaniment to dinner, try putting a phone with tunes on it in an empty ceramic mug.

Happy Camper Tip #18

Frannie's Mandarin Orange Cake: Preheat oven to 350 °. In a large bowl, combine the following:

2 1/2 cups of flour, 1 3/4 cups sugar, 2 teaspoons baking powder, 1 1/2 teaspoons baking soda, 1/4 teaspoons. salt, 2 eggs, 2 teaspoons vanilla, 1 15 oz. can of

mandarin oranges (undrained) OR 1 small can and two Clementines, 1 cup of walnut pieces, 1 teaspoon cinnamon, 1/2 teaspoon cloves.

Beat at medium speed for two minutes. Pour into greased 9 x 13 pan and bake for 35-40 minutes.

Topping: While cake is baking, combine the following in a small saucepan: 3/4 cup brown sugar, packed, 3 tablespoons butter, 3 tablespoons milk, and 1/2 teaspoons vanilla. Cook over medium heat and boil for two minutes. Pour over cake immediately after removing from the oven.

Good with whipped topping; excellent with lemon custard ice cream.

Happy Camper Tip #19

I have mentioned before the wealth of local museums and festivals but it seems worth repeating. Almost every town seems to have at least one old home, depot, school, or church that has been turned into a museum, historical site, retail store or tourist bureau. On our camping trips we have toured old barns, the bridges of Madison County, wineries, and the Surf Ballroom, scene of the last Buddy Holly concert. There are also birthplaces of famous people, caves, and other attractions and the Internet makes them easy to find. Unless you look for the covered bridges after a couple of roads have washed out. But that's another story.

Happy Camper Tip #20

Mickey's Shrimp Boil:

½ cup Old Bay Seasoning, 2 tablespoons salt, 4 quarts water, 1 (12 ounce) can beer, 8 medium red potatoes, cut in quarters, 2 large vidalia onions, cut in wedges, 2 lbs smoked sausage, cut in 2 inch lengths, 8 ears frozen corn on the cob, thawed, 4 lbs large shrimp, in shells

In a turkey fryer, bring Old Bay, salt, water and beer to a boil. Add potatoes and onions; cook over high heat for 8 minutes. Add smoked sausage; continue to cook on high for 5 minutes. Add corn to pot; continue to boil for 7 minutes. Add shrimp in shells, cook for 4 minutes. Drain cooking liquid; pour contents of pot into several large bowl or shallow pails.

Sprinkle with additional Old Bay.

Happy Camper Tip #21

Rhubarb Dream Bars:

Crust: 2 cups flour, 3/4 cup powdered sugar, 1 cup butter

Mix crust and press into 9 x 13 pan. Bake in 350° oven for 15 minutes.

Filling: 4 beaten eggs, 4 cups chopped rhubarb, 2 cups sugar, 1/4 cup flour, 1/2 teaspoon salt

Combine eggs, sugar, flour, and salt and mix well. Fold in rhubarb. Pour on top of baked crust. Bake for 40-55 minutes until set and edges start to brown.

Happy Camper Tip #22

Burgers And Dogs Cupcakes: Make cupcakes in your favorite flavor. Frost with white frosting and add sprinkles. For the burgers, place a Keebler's mint cookie on a vanilla wafer. Red and yellow frosting can be used for ketchup and mustard and sprinkles of green tinted coconut looks like shredded lettuce. Top with another vanilla wafer, brush with a little frozen orange juice and sprinkle with sesame seed. Place on top of the cupcake.

For hot dogs, slice a marshmallow circus peanut part way through and mold a hot dog shape out of a caramel. Top with 'ketchup' and 'mustard.'

Happy Camper Tip #23:

Insulation: Most trailers and RVs are not insulated the way a house is. If you travel in the winter you can benefit from a couple of simple tricks. Vent insulators, or vent cushions, are available from RV stores, simply push into the vent area, and prevent the loss of precious heat. They can also be used in the summer to keep direct sun out when using the AC.

Windows are always a prominent cause of heat loss. Bubble wrap—the larger the bubbles, the better—can be cut to fit the window glass, sprayed with water, and smoothed over the glass until no longer needed.

Happy Camper Tip #24:

Noodles to Protect Your Noodle: Foam noodles are useful to prevent injuries if you put them on awning braces or any kind of tie downs.

Happy Camper Tip #25

Backbone State Park: Dolomite State Park is based on Backbone, Iowa's first state park and one of the most popular. It is located between Strawberry Point and Dundee, Iowa and is about 2000 acres.There are cabins for rent as well as 125 campsites. The Civilian Conservation Corps in the 1930s built the dam on the Maquoketa River that forms Backbone Lake, the unique bath house, and cabins, as well as roads and restrooms. Twenty-one miles of trails includes the famous 'Devil's Backbone' Trail along a high ridge of rock.

The Iowa Civilian Conservation Corps (CCC) Museum opened in 1990 and is located just within the park's west gate. It provides visitors with an interesting and informative look at the work of the CCC in Iowa state parks. Backbone was the site of two CCC camps and contains many buildings and structures built by the CCC. The museum is open on weekends Memorial Day through Labor Day and by special arrangement through the park office.

ACKNOWLEDGMENTS

We were introduced to the world of geocaching by our camping friends, the Ottaways, and, while not diehards, have enjoyed this activity, especially when camping with the grandkids. Thanks!

Thank you also to my readers who submitted camping hints and recipes. And to my great beta readers, Elaine, Marcia, and Ginge.

I cannot ignore, though, the campers who provide so much material for campground humor. I have included nothing that we haven't seen or done.

ABOUT THE AUTHOR

Karen Musser Nortman is the author of the Frannie Shoemaker Campground cozy mystery series, including the BRAGMedallion honoree, *Bats and Bones*. After previous incarnations as a secondary social studies teacher (22 years) and a test developer (18 years), she returned to her childhood dream of writing a novel. The Frannie Shoemaker Campground Mysteries came out of numerous 'round the campfire' discussions, making up answers to questions raised by the peephole glimpses one gets into the lives of fellow campers. Where did those people disappear to for the last two days? What kinds of bones are in this fire pit? Why is that woman wearing heels to the shower house?

Karen and her husband Butch originally tent camped when their children were young and switched to a travel trailer when sleeping on the ground lost its romantic adventure. They take frequent weekend jaunts with friends to parks in Iowa and surrounding states, plus occasional longer trips. Entertainment on these trips has ranged from geocaching and hiking/biking to barbecue contests, balloon fests, and buck skinners' rendezvous.

Sign up for Karen's email list at www.karenmussernortman.com and receive a free ereader download of The Blue Coyote..

OTHER BOOKS BY THE AUTHOR

THE AWARD-WINNING FRANNIE SHOEMAKER CAMPGROUND MYSTERIES:

Bats and Bones: (An IndieBRAG Medallion honoree) Frannie and Larry Shoemaker are retirees who enjoy weekend camping with their friends in state parks. They anticipate the usual hiking, campfires, good food, and interesting side trips among the bluffs of beautiful Bat Cave State Park for the long Fourth of July weekend—until a dead body turns up. Confined in the campground and surrounded by strangers, Frannie is drawn into the investigation. Frannie's persistence and curiosity helps authorities sort through the possible suspects and motives, but almost ends her new sleuth career—and her life—for good.

The Blue Coyote: (An IndieBRAG Medallion honoree and a 2013 Chanticleer CLUE finalist) Frannie and Larry Shoemaker love taking their grandchildren, Sabet and Joe, camping with them. But at Bluffs State Park, Frannie finds herself worrying more than usual about their safety, and when another young girl disappears from the campground in broad daylight, her fears increase. The fun of a bike ride, a flea market, marshmallow guns, and a storyteller are quickly overshadowed. Accusations against Larry and her add to the cloud over their heads.

Peete and Repeat: (An IndieBRAG Medallion honoree, 2013 Chanticleer CLUE finalist, and 2014 Chanticleer Mystery and Mayhem finalist) A biking and camping trip to southeastern Minnesota turns into double trouble for Frannie Shoemaker and her friends as she deals with a canoeing mishap and a couple of bodies. Strange happenings in the campground, the nearby nature learning center, and an old power plant complicate the suspect pool and Frannie tries to stay out of it--really--but what can she do?

The Lady of the Lake: (An IndieBRAG Medallion honoree, 2014 Chanticleer CLUE finalist) A trip down memory lane is fine if you don't stumble on a body. Frannie Shoemaker and her friends camp at Old Dam Trail State Park near one of Donna Nowak's childhood homes. They take in the county fair, reminisce at a Fifties-Sixties dance, and check out old hangouts. But the present intrudes when a body surfaces. Donna becomes the focus of the investigation and Frannie wonders if the police shouldn't be looking closer at the victim's many enemies. A traveling goddess worshipper, a mystery writer and the Sisters on the Fly add color to the campground.

THE TIME TRAVEL TRAILER SERIES

The Time Travel Trailer: A 1937 vintage camper trailer half hidden in weeds catches Lynne McBriar's eye when she is visiting an elderly friend Ben. Ben eagerly sells it to her and she just as eagerly embarks on a restoration. But after each remodel, sleeping in the trailer lands Lynne and her daughter Dinah in a previous decade—exciting, yet frightening. Glimpses of their home town and ancestors fifty or sixty years earlier is exciting and also offers some clues to the mystery of Ben's lost love. But when Dinah makes a trip on her own, separating herself from her mother by decades, Lynne has never known such fear. It is a trip that may upset the future if Lynne and her estranged husband can't team up to bring their daughter back.

CPSIA information can be obtained
at www.ICGtesting.com
Printed in the USA
LVOW03s2240180118

563141LV00005B/837/P